Shocking Pink by Ananda Lowe

G000098782

Chapter Twelve; The Truth

Heaven

Bleeding Rainbows

The pen beckons full of red ink. It writes a

story of disillusionment. I stare at the light

reflecting off the shards of a smashed

prism,

                                                bleeding

rainbows,

And hallucinates events in history; soldiers raising arms, Romans in skirts, Greeks, Vikings,

Celts with severed heads attached to their belts, like talismans,

Dripping brains like sawdust, in their chipboard chariots.

                        Am I chasing smoke through two-way

mirrors?

Chapter One: The Search Begins

I sell my *smartphone* to a cool looking man in original Nike trainers for fifty pounds, and this allows me to buy a ticket for the coach to the West Country. As well as procuring a poetry book from the charity shop for the journey, I bought a casual hoodie and some dark-blue skinny-jeans to wear with my grey canvas shoes. I get on the coach at Victoria. I am glad to leave. I sit by the window and place my small rucksack possessing all my worldly belongings on the floor by my feet.

The engine starts and I watch The Suitcase People scurrying around as we pull away from London and drive through the busy streets. An old woman with white hair peers over at me from her seat opposite. If I live long enough to be considered old, I'd keep my hair really short and maybe dye it bright colours to be original. The queen would suit bright turquoise hair, she wouldn't require her multitude of hats then, though I don't think space is a problem in her dwelling.

I read. Then I shut my eyes and try to sleep but am plagued with thoughts of the coach crashing, hearing the screams of people dying. Since the loss of my partner, my life is like a permanent nightmare. When we arrive, I watch the old woman getting off, discussing sun cream and her nieces and nephews, bless her. I wish my life could be filled with such mundane things. I move along the aisle.

'Thank you,' I say to the driver as I step down off the new coach; like a space shuttle on wheels, with mirrors either side of the windscreen which looks like a giant bee's antennae.

The door electronically slides to the side with a hiss. I am in Bristol in the afternoon. As I descend and go through the bay into the bus station, I notice a scruffy homeless man smoking outside the primarily glass building. He has a giant rucksack on his back and looks overloaded. He throws his roll up on the floor and enters the building with a can of lager hidden up one sleeve, as he passes, he looks at me. I muster up all my courage to go and stand beside him. I will initiate a conversation with this man, he may be able to help me.

'You look a bit lost,' he declares, 'what're you doing waiting around bus stations?'

'I've nowhere else to go I suppose,' I answer sadly.

We stand talking by four huge clocks with lit up faces and long slender arms, each one pointing to different times of the day. These clocks are attached to the floor, as if they have each been rolled into their positions by a giant and stretched across the back-glass wall. This is my first encounter of a street-person in Bristol.

'My name's Sara by the way.'

'Squirrel,' he replies.

We chat for a while; I explain that I have nowhere to sleep and won't go into detail. He is jovial and tries to make me laugh. We have a mutual love of animals and nature. He is grubby but nice.

'Do you want to come for a pipe in the toilets to cheer you up?' He enquires. 'We can go in the females; they have more cubicles.'

'Okay,' I answer and follow him. The public toilets are nearby. We go in through a turnstile.

There's no romance here. The bright fluorescent light glares back, illuminating the stark reality; like wearing glasses where the strong lenses create such a clear picture that the lines are sharp enough to cut. My initial time in this city and I'm sitting with this scraggly stranger, only just on a first name basis, on the floor of a cubicle in the small public conveniences; he has just moved his rucksack to make a space. I notice that Squirrel has a tattoo on his arm of an anarchist symbol.

'Fuck the system,' Squirrel declares, noticing me staring at this, 'and fuck God.'

I explore the man's, Squirrel's, face whilst he sits on the closed-lidded toilet before me; his creased, weathered features, his ginger goatee, and bloodshot eyes with the slightly vacant, drink-induced, look. How many brain cells have deliberately escaped out of his head by being ejected in his foamy-bile-vomit? Yet, he is kind after all and what have people done with their valued I.Q's; maybe, in his nihilistic stupor, this man's intellect is superior to everyone because he knows that humans are the locusts of the earth and treats himself accordingly. Or maybe I'm suffering from depression like Doctor Hansel said, he also commented that it was strange to experience this in someone so young and my state of mind must be inextricably linked to the death of my partner.

Squirrel says, 'I'll try and find us somewhere to stay for tonight if you want Sara.'

'Yes, that would be good, thanks.'

Squirrel's in his thirties; his bloodshot eyes are green with brown flecks in them, and he has reddish hair in long matted dreadlocks. I trust him. Most people would think I'm mad, but he emanates a muted light. The lines on his face make him appear interesting.

He has a small ball of Cling film and is starting to unwrap this, complaining while he's doing so; 'bloody crack dealers, they wrap so much Cling film around it in case they have to swallow it if they're stopped by the police.'

When he finally reaches the contents inside, I notice that it is small and white, like a tiny stone. Squirrel extracts a black box from the front pocket of the rucksack sandwiched between his legs. The box reveals a pipe. The pipe's similarly to the wooden pipe of an old man but is made of glass and is smaller. Squirrel carefully places the crumbs of the drug in the bowl which is filled with wire wool.

There's a flick of a lighter, a crackle, as the stuff in the pipe bubbles and melts. Squirrel exhales voluminous smoke. It's hard to see through the rising smokescreen. Everything feels so alien. He carefully passes me the reloaded pipe. I justify using this drug by the fact that I need to *fit in* with this man, I am homeless and on my own and need friends. I've never done this before. I feel a strange disconnection from my actions, as if someone else is doing them, I have felt this way since my partner passed away, I'm insensate to life, almost as if I'm only half alive.

I take the pipe. I inhale as Squirrel holds the flame over the bowl end. I stop inhaling and cough. The taste is hard to describe. Even though it tastes of chemicals, this is nice. I put on my metaphorical, pink-tinted sunglasses, ready to be worn again when the real world gets too much for me to handle, night and day,

My mouth goes numb, and I can't speak. I feel good. I feel high. I like everything; the surroundings and the company I am in. I feel like Squirrel is my brother and everything is achievable. I'm in the right place at the right time. Even though my mouth feels numb, I chat easily with my new-found-friend, the barriers have been removed and I feel cool; like there is an intensity in the surroundings which is electric.

'It's strong stuff,' Squirrel advises me. 'I'll do some begging later and we can get some more. I can get some brown as well,' he smiles again and holds out his grubby hand for me to give back the pipe.

He returns this into the black box which he replaces back in his rucksack. He then gets out a piece of tin foil, which he opens out, there's a flat foil-tube inside, he reshapes this round a pencil which he has obviously acquired from Argos. I can see black lines on the main piece with a shiny brown blob in the middle. He holds the lighter under this and funnels the smoke through the tube and into his lungs. It smells like fish heads and rubber.

'What's brought you to Bristol?' Squirrel asks, taking a break and looking at me intently.

'I wanted to go somewhere new,' I reply.

'Do you want a line,' Squirrel offers, passing the foil to me, 'what's the matter, you must have seen heroin before,' he says, noticing my eyes widening.

'Erm...yes of course I have,' I tug the foil out of his grasp.

'I'll run it for you,' Squirrel says, his speech has slowed down, and he looks different. He keeps closing his eyes and rubbing his nose and face with his hand. His ginger dreadlocks obscuring his vision. 'Breathe in as much as possible and hold it in like you did with the crack,' he advises.

I do, trying not to cough at the rancid taste.

'Pass it back,' Squirrel orders and takes back the foil and tube, possessively.

'Have you any idea where we're going to sleep tonight?' I ask, in a comfortable haze of contentment, forgetting that I'm sitting with a relative stranger on the cubicle floor. I feel warm.

'Don't worry,' Squirrel answers, 'we'll be okay.'

Squirrel starts to make a roll up out of fag butts he has collected in a worn and scratched tobacco tin. When he finishes, he rises up and slings his big steel-reinforced-rucksack over his shoulder and stoops slightly because of the weight of this.

'Come on, let's go, first, we should get some food from the soup-run in the underpass, it's only a minute away. I'll introduce you to some of my friends there,' he announces. 'They might know of a squat where we can stay tonight, otherwise it may have to be the shelter, or if it isn't cold, outside in the park.'

We leave through the turnstiles which remind me of the ones in tube stations; Squirrel marches in front of me, stomping in his army boots, with his frizzy matted mane. Out in the bus station, people sit on benches by different bays waiting for buses and others are buying stuff from the kiosk. We turn and leave by the glass-automatic-doors and Squirrel lights up his roll up. I surveyed my new home.

A huge twenty-storied building is across the small road and looms above me with a sign saying Premier Inn, taunting me due to my lack of funds to be able to check into such a place. Next Door to this is a modern, one-storey church. It has a lit sign with a crown and Jesus's name on it, like a fast-food shop. On the right, the road becomes a dead end, the middle automatic-doors of the station come out onto paving, with benches either side, and, as I look up, a steeple of another older church meets my eyes with a gold cockerel on the top glistening in the sun and arrows showing the cardinal points. This is a good landmark to remember.

We go left and all around me high-rises sprout out of the concrete and stretch to the sky. We cross the road to some railings and a small set of steps takes us down to the top level of a tiny mall. In the open middle, two lamp posts rise up from the ground over my head. We take the steps down to the lower level and see an abstract, multi-coloured piece of graffiti on the wall of one of the vacant shops, and on the other side is a tunnel, lit with rectangular lights running along one side. The walls are covered in white tiles.

We go through the tunnel into a paved area, lower than the surrounding roads, with rectangular flower beds in the middle and sloping banks of grass rising to the outer walls. This has five tunnels leading off in different directions; obviously leading through to a slope or steps that take you up to the pavements on each side. I pass another piece of graffiti, violet, pink and blue flowers on red brick. Another Brick In The Wall. Squirrel stops and takes out a gold can from his bag and gulps the contents down as we stroll on, and then crushes the can and slings this into one of the old-heavy-iron-bins. I can hear a busker with his guitar singing in one of the other tunnels across from us.

We join a huddle of homeless people in the middle of the underpass; all standing around waiting to be fed. These are the walking wounded; old men shake as they drink their cider, occasionally stopping to swear or spit. Others are sitting talking to themselves. It looks like these people have survived a nuclear war, looking deformed and discoloured. This would scare me, but Squirrel and I have put on my metaphorical, pink-tinted sunglasses and everything has metamorphosed. The world has transmuted, the sun is now a golden corral, dark colours have more depth, light colours glow, and people look full of vitality.

Approaching the group, I realise that they're crowding around a camping table with receptacles. A lady standing behind this is sporting a T-shirt which says Jesus loves us. *Does it take religion to persuade people to care about one another?* In our capitalist society do we require religious belief systems to equalise individuals' prospects. The lady hands out the food whilst discussing the bible to a man beside her. Squirrel has drifted over to some people sitting nearby, he glances over and smiles at me, and I reciprocate.

'I just have to talk to a friend of mine,' Squirrel calls over to me, he's standing by a low wall which provides seating. 'Go and get some food and come over. I'll get mine in a bit.'

I get in line, waiting for my turn. When it arrives, the smiling lady ladles me out a polystyrene plate of food and twists the nozzle on the flask so coffee runs into my polystyrene cup. I add sugar out of the Tupperware container with the plastic spoon provided.

'Thank you,' I say.

'Dats okay darling,' the lady replies, 'de food is nice, it's one of mi Jamaican recipes, meat stew with rice an dumpling. Yu go an eat it up now while it's hot, do yu hear. Mi names is Sister Pauline, pleased to meet yu.'

I weave in and out of the crowd, trying not to spill my coffee. I can smell sweat, earth and stale alcohol. I join Squirrel and sit on the wall, thinking the food will probably just taste of polystyrene; I am wrong, it's okay, it isn't a meal at the Jamie Oliver restaurant but it's more than adequate. I eat while surveying the events around me with a clinical eye.

A good-looking man is talking very loudly near me. They all talk loudly. I feel like I am in a classroom full of kids with attention-deficit-disorder. I listen to his conversation, 'bloody Mickey went over again, stupid twat, in it. He was dead for two minutes. I'm sure he is trying to kill himself, in it. The paramedics had to give him a shot in the neck of adrenaline,' the speaker stops to take a swig of his beer and then returns to his tale, 'he was well pissed off. He said it was the best buzz he ever had till they brought him round, in it. The only thing he cared about when he came to was whether his hair looked alright, in it, his baseball cap had come off, he got up and started to shape his hair in the mirror in front of the paramedics.' The man listening to the story burst out laughing. 'I felt like punching Mickey in the head, in it. I had to apologise for him, in it,' the storytellers friends laugh raucously.

Another sallow faced lad in a baseball cap approaches them, interrupting the story, 'Innit, have you seen, Rene?'

The storyteller, I now know to be Innit, replies, 'just been talking about you Mickey, speak of The Devil and he will appear, in it.'

So, this narrator's name is Innit. This is a funny world. Instead of talking about getting drunk, they are discussing death as if it is as normal as a hang-over. Their regard for human life must be so far removed from any average person's. These are damaged individuals. Maybe that is why I am here, I should fit straight in, I haven't been the same since my partner's death.

Innit replies, 'Mickey I ain't seen, Rene. You know where she goes, in it. If you need her, go and look for her, in it.'

Innit is sitting with his group of friends on the small wall across from us. Squirrel calls Innit over to where we are sitting, I hear my name and realise that he's introducing me, 'Sara, this is, Innit. I know he looks strange but he's a good person to know.' Innit thumps him on the arm playfully.

After this introduction, Squirrel goes to get his food; leaving me to become acquainted with Innit. I have another mouthful of food and leave the rest, shutting the polystyrene lid and placing the container on the grass bank behind me.

'Hello,' I say, noticing the man for the first time.

He's around my age and is typically dressed in jeans and red T-shirt, with a black hoodie tied around his waist, unlike Squirrel who's wearing a holey Adicts T-shirt (a punk band), combat trousers and army boots. Innit is scruffy and unwashed, with tattoos on his knuckles and slightly puffy hands, but he's handsome and has nice brown eyes, with long eyelashes, and longish blonde hair.

'Alright,' Innit answers and sits down on the wall beside me, ' I hear you're new in Bristol and Squirrel here is helping you out, in it. Any friend of Squirrel's is a friend of mine.'

'Thanks, that's good to know, I don't know anyone here except Squirrel.'

'Well, you know me now,' Innit smiles. 'I'm not sure if that's a good or a bad thing, in it,' he laughs. 'Only joking, if anyone gives you any bother just come and tell me or Squirrel,' Innit advises, being genuine and trying to impress me with his alpha-male stance. 'In fact, don't bother talking to anyone else,' he specifies, 'hang with us and you'll be fine, in it.'

Squirrel returns with his plate of food. 'Give me some space,' he orders to Innit who obediently shuffles closer towards me. Squirrel sits down to eat. He takes a few mouthfuls, and his cheeks bulge out at the sides; his jaw makes a clicking sound.

'Squirrel, why are you called that?' I ask.

He finishes his mouthful and replies, 'because the red squirrel is endangered; I name myself Squirrel as homage to them,' he smiles, 'I'm the red-haired Squirrel.'

'Don't you mean you're a ginger cunt, in it,' Innit responds, laughing. I can't help but laugh as well.

'Your hair is a reddish chestnut colour,' I add, looking at Squirrel.

'Did you hear that, Innit?' Squirrel asks, smiling, holding his plastic fork poised to dig into his rice and chicken.

'Yeah, respek Bruv, in it,' Innit smiles and touches fists with Squirrel in an American gang style handshake, 'what're we doing then? Are you going to finish your food, or do you want me to eat it, in it?'

Squirrel shovels in the last few mouthfuls and ditches the plate on the floor. 'Right, I need to make money,' Squirrel proclaims decisively, 'I thought I'd leave you two in Castle Park for a while, is that okay with you both? Sara, what do you reckon?'

'That's fine, Squirrel,' I answer, feeling a bit apprehensive, 'can we meet you at a certain time somewhere?'

Squirrel must have sensed my trepidation because he replies, ' I'm going to get you both to wander up to my *begging-spot*, that way if you two lose each other, you know where I am Sara.'

'Can you beg me up a couple of pounds so I can get a bottle of cider, In it?' Innit asks in his usual vernacular language and stands up.

'Yeah,' Squirrel responds, 'you'll have to wait with me till I get the money, it shouldn't take that long.' Squirrel is astute, I could tell that if he really concentrated on something he would achieve good results which is reassuring.

'Yes, yes. Come then you two, in it,' Innit says, looking down at us.

Chapter Two; The Search Continues

We trail along behind Squirrel. I compare Innit's and Squirrel's walk. Squirrel has a small wiry frame and looks like his body is moulded around a giant bowling ball, Innit on the other hand keeps his head up and back straight, he's tall which helps to establish the impression that he is worth something despite his dirty appearance. We take the tunnel to the left of us, the tunnels all seem to have big painted canvases along one side, or the two I've been through have, but this one has a canvas which catches my eye, it has a purple background with patterns and writing in black over the top, the writing says 'be the change you want to see' with the name Gandhi beneath this quote. I'd read online that Gandhi didn't say this, but the premise of what he said is analogous. We all know who he is, like Jesus, another renowned person with good stuff to say. They both died for their beliefs. Life seems to castigate people sometimes. I know the spirit of Jesus still comes and saves people, so people say.

Sorry to all the people who take faith seriously, I have a healthy respect for religion and realise that the word God is an embodiment of a force, or energy, that no one understands. To believe in God and Jesus is not so weird when we have scientists saying we are all a projection from a giant black hole, which can't be true because we have eclipses. There is more to life than just the external dimension, there is an inner dimension, we all are connected. The philosopher Jung called this a 'collective unconscious', which he stated is reflected in our dream worlds. He also said that this collective unconscious could openly be called God and is a superior source of wisdom. I would rename this the universal consciousness. I'd never craved money like most, I craved the answer to the meaning of life and the universe.

Anyway, I go up the stairs, passing a randomly placed big mural of a brown bear, and onto the pavement leading under a multi-storied building. I later find out that the name for the underpass is The Bear Pit, it is home to many homeless who use the tunnels as a dry place to sleep or put-up tents on the grass banks. In the Bible it states that 'my father's house has many rooms', where are the rooms for all the people here? Sorry to use such a common Bible quote but the rising amount of homeless people does question the validity of this.

I am in an enclosed walkway either side of the busy, dual-carriage road. Squirrel trudges along beside me, lugging his rucksack. This arched walkway has a big circular window made of clear plastic separating the pavement from the road. The plastic's written on and scorched, the view of the road is unclear. We come out from beneath the building, past the bus stop, and cross at the pelican crossing, standing in the middle island and noticing a stencil of an astronaut holding carrier bags on the building opposite. I examine everything around me with interest.

'We're now on Gloucester Road,' Squirrel enlightens me as we trek uphill. Even though Squirrel looks rough and uncared for, there is something nice about him. Like I said before, his honesty shines through his eyes. He is funny and intelligent, if somewhat obscured by alcohol which makes him appear slightly *Punch Drunk* on occasions. We stomp along chatting like good friends.

I ask Squirrel, 'when did you become homeless?'

He answers, 'I've been this way for as long as I can remember. I've never had a real home.' Squirrel turns into Pinocchio in front of me saying 'I want to be a real boy', I shake the image out of my head as he continues, 'I was in Care homes and kept running away.

They'd take me back at first, but they soon gave up and left me to my own devices,' he sounds disconnected, as if he is talking about someone else.

The busy shopping street runs uphill, graffiti is everywhere. We pass a lit-up amusement arcade and further up, across the road, I see graffiti writing on the front of a shop saying 'Massages'. I'd like one of those right now. I notice a lot of graffiti as I plod along; all the walls are covered in scribbled names. The number of sprayed words makes my head feel confused and messy, but the actual artworks are inspiring in places. The streets are like canvases for anyone with something to say, 'the words of the prophets are written on the subway walls'.

Squirrel nods hello to a man drinking Special Brew, in camouflage clothes, with brightly coloured hair, walking alongside a loose dog. If my mum were here, she would say 'people like that don't deserve animals'. She is limited in her outlook sometimes; actually, he seems like a good dog owner. His dog appears well fed, happy and is bounding along by his side. The man pats his dog on the head affectionately and then glances at me with interest.

I need to get my bearings, so make a mental note of points of significance. As we reach a turning on our left, I see a revolving advertisement in front of us. The sunlight is beautiful. I look across from me, and just down from the revolving advertisement I can see a big church. The church has been built in a traditional design but is made from modern materials; it looks odd. Squirrel slows his pace right down. On our side of the road, a man is spray-painting pictures on two windows of what I assume is a red-brick office-buildings. He's painted the windows black primarily, blocking out the sunshine for the office-workers inside. Further down, I can see another graffitied up building. Squirrel slows his pace right down.

'Why are you slowing down?' I query, I didn't want to lose him, he is my introduction into this unorthodox way of life and the people within it.

'Because I'm almost at my *begging-spot*,' he declares. 'It's out of the centre so I'm less likely to be seen by the police. If they see me, they will arrest me, rough me up and take my money for the Police Widows Fund,' Squirrel explains.

Carrying on a little way up the road, we see a building which looks like it was built in the seventies with benches and tables outside and a weird sign on the front. Squirrel sits down and put on a persona of vulnerability.

'This spot is a good earner,' Squirrel explains, 'I'll get that two pound for you, Innit.'

Squirrel is sitting in front of a bar. As I wait, I study the bar. The square tables, out front, consist of plywood with painted patterns on the tops and accompanying small grey chairs with big, closed, orange parasols above them. The front outside-seating-area has walls of penning in the seats and tables. These walls are painted with pictures.

One wall to the right has a picture of a big bear throwing a Malakoff cocktail at three stencilled riot-police. The words 'Mild Mild West' are at the top and 'Banksy', the name of the artist, is written at the bottom. I'm familiar with the notorious Banksy, his stencilled paintings sold for thousands in upmarket art galleries. It's interesting to see Banksy's roots.

This bar is aptly called The Canteen with cool people sitting outside. A low wall separates the seating area from the pavement, with flower beds running along this with cables affixed to posts to support the weight of the numerous plants, including big orange sunflowers. The plants block out the eyesore of the main road.

Standing on the other side of the wall, I look through a gap in the plants and see that the bar has glass doors all the way along, you can see right through to the bar running along the back wall which has mirrors and shelves containing bottles of all different coloured liquids. Outside, a big dog Is milling free in-between the tables and chairs. The owner sits with her back to me. All I can see is her bright pink hair.

The people in this bar will have to pass Squirrel sitting cross-legged with his back against the wall. He's next to a line of numerous bikes locked up on the railings provided. Another man is begging across the road, I feel as if I am in the internal war of the classes with the casualties.

Squirrel gives the change to Innit, ' right...go... they give you more money when you're on your own. I should have at least fifty quid by ten o'clock. They give more change when they're drunk.'

'Be careful,' I say, genuinely apprehensive.

'Don't worry,' he answers.

I leave him still asking passers-by for spare change. I don't feel embarrassed like I should, I'm talking to a beggar. I feel a strange sort of detachment from *normal* society, like wearing a cloak of invisibility. Squirrel and Innit are cavalier about the situation, and

they make this seem natural and I feel at ease with it. I shouldn't
do, but I do. I'm studying my new environment with interest. I want
to be a published writer, so I need to be able to recall details of my
observations. I retrace my steps and head downhill along the main
road with,
Innit.

There's a middle-aged man dancing further up the main road, with
headphones on, in the central part of a pelican crossing, he's
wearing a bright high-visibility top with 'Jesus Saves' written on the
back. No one seems surprised, as if this is completely routine. I
retrace my steps and head downhill along the main road with Innit.

Innit turns his head to face me and says, 'come, let's go and sit
down by the river in the centre, in it, we've nothing else to do, in
it.'

'Don't you need to make some money? I ask.

'No, in it. Squirrel is going to go halves with me on some stuff, I
sorted him out the other day so it's his turn, in it. We can both sort
you out, in it.'

'Oh,' I say. 'You don't have to do that,' I genuinely mean it. The
thought of doing more drugs scares me, and at the same time, I
want to do them again. I like the feeling.

'We don't have to, but we will, in it.' Innit says, thinking he is
doing me a favour, nothing is more erroneous. The stuff they are
talking about is not going to do anyone any favours.

He pulls me up. We cross at traffic lights and go up into the
newsagents to buy a bottle of white cider. We go back along
Jamaica street and see a corner house covered in graffiti; the red
and white background of a giant wave, like a tsunami, conceals the
front door, and a comic character is sitting on the shoulders of

another on stilts with a microscope reflecting a huge eye out of the top lens, this reaches right up to the second-floor window.

A stencil of a panda is beneath a signpost for the road which turns down to join with Gloucester Road. We emerge by the hospital and walk until we meet up with a road leading downhill. We swing right and pass the Bristol theatre (The Hippodrome) and the water feature, which is a large rectangular shallow pool with jets of water shooting out in arcs at different measured points, this is placed on a central island surrounded by main roads, offices and pubs, and a statue of Neptune, another of a man dressed like a character from a Dickens novel which I learn is Mr Cabot, who, like many men from his time was a slave trader, he probably did good as well but this fact shadows his memory, and I see a war memorial further along.

After a twenty-minute trudge along nameless streets, we arrived at Castle Park. Everything's alien to me. I presume the park is called this because amidst the green banks, trees and bushes is a castle with a tower and small slat windows. We clamber up one bank, going under some of the trees, and see two squirrels dancing about with red heads, grey bodies, and funny kinks at the top of their tails, one scrabbles up the tree trunk and is perfectly camouflaged. Between the sloping banks are paths leading through to the river. We go down a path, stopping halfway along to sit on a bench. We pass the bottle of sweet fizzy liquid between us until only the dregs are left, which I decline gracefully. The bench is comfortable; the surface has worn down and become grainy through age.

I watch the boat called Matilda chug by on the river with the sun reflecting off the surface. To the right is a path leading down to a wooden jetty where you can moor your boats at water level, a houseboat is floating in the water slightly down from the jetty and is literally a house on a floating platform, with a slate roof, windows and a front door. I would like to own this right now. A bridge for cars to drive across is further along.

When I look left, I see another bridge giving cars access across the river on the opposite side. The smell of the sea lingers in the air which is strange considering we're by the river. I imagine a holiday in the south of France, I can hear the waves, I almost have to shade my eyes from the sun and can taste the cocktails with the mixture of fruit juices and spirits, mostly brightly coloured, I am sucking on my straw, playing with my slice of orange and stirring the ice around the glass. I wish.

On the left is a path leading through arches of office buildings, on the horizon is a huge modern tower on this side with the words 'Bristol.co.uk' written sideways up the tower, and three metal steeples on separate buildings, two with crosses on the top, one of them is attached to the castle tower. The castle's main building's stained-glass windows are obscured in places by leaves. Bristol, I am in Bristol of all places, there are some beautiful parts of this city, so I have been told; Bristol Cathedral and The Harbourside. I had friends that used to live here and divulged that there is a tower called Cabot Tower in the park where you can view the entirety of the city.

Across from us is a riverside development and the noise of the drill, or stone cutter, is filling the air. The front of a tall building has wooden frames for the windows but no glass and no other walls or floors, you can see through the front windows to the next building; this is metaphorically representative of my life right now. A massive crane is on top of a tall building beside this development and is like a metal arm with a pirate's hook. Innit crushes the empty cider bottle and throws it into a nearby bin.

Innit goes over to lean on the railings in front of the river. 'Have you noticed how most people traipse around like zombies in their nine to five jobs, in it? They never really see what's around them, in it.' Innit calls me over. 'Sara, watch the patterns the water makes, in it.' Innit, I'm finding out, is deeper than he looks. He walks back over to the bench I'm sitting on. 'Living *out* gets you to notice the little things, in it,' he announces.

'Yeah great,' I say, sarcastically and roll my eyes up to the sky. I'd much rather have a home. I get up and gaze out at the river to see the patterns he's talking about. The slight breeze starts to tangle my plaited hair, so I pull my hood up. The water has perfectly spaced, wavy lines that ripple and look dappled in places. The sun reflects off the water like glistening snakes that are weaving in and out, flanking each other. The water shimmers beautifully. I understand Innit's interest in the natural world.

My life feels like this water as it flows freely. The only trouble is that dates and times and organisation make me feel safe, I like predictability, a framework in my life that formulates my sanity. I'd have to style my own routine. I'm glad Innit is here for company and that I have a friend.

'Sara, tell me about yourself, where did you grow up? Have you got any brothers or sisters, what led to you being here in it?

'It's a long story.' I say.

'We have time, in it. It ain't like we have anywhere to go,' Innit responds.

'I grew up in the countryside near Camberley ...and I live, I mean lived with my partner in London,' I felt and sounded uncomfortable saying this.

'You are no longer together? you can tell me Sara,' Innit responds, sitting down beside me, putting one foot up on the bench.

'He d-died,' I stammered, knitting my hands together in my lap, 'my partner and I were remarkably close,'.

Innit responds, 'sorry if this is upsetting for you, in it.'

I reply, 'can we change the subject.'

'Cool, don't worry,' Innit replies, 'I have lost people too. I got split up from my sister and brother when we went into Care, haven't seen them since they were both really young, in it, I was left on the streets because of being older, not so easy to rehome, I had been looking after them from babies in it,' Innit starts to run his hands through his greasy hair.

'Sorry Innit.' I say and give him a hug, trying not to show how bothered I am by how dirty he is.

We drop the subject. Innit can relate to my pain, this is good to know. I look into his nice brown eyes; I'm starting to feel tipsy from the white cider. My cheeks are warm. Tonight, I'm set to sleep in the bushes with relative strangers, talk about living dangerously, all I can do is trust my instincts, which are saying that these men are okay. I've a rape alarm in my pocket and I'd keep this in reach at all times.

I see a group of people sitting in a tight circle up on one of the banks which is sheltered by bushes and trees, one is playing guitar, so we drift over.

'Come and join us,' the guitarist says, a good-looking lad with longish hair and casual clothes. 'Do you want a smoke?' he asks and offers me a spliff. When I take this, he smiles.

'Thanks,' I reply.

'My name's James,' the guitarist reveals.

'I'm Sara, and this is Innit.'

'You remind me of someone,' James states.

'I only arrived in Bristol today.'

'Oh,' James looks bemused, 'I can't place where I've seen you before. Anyway, there's a party tomorrow night, come, it'll be good. A friend's sound system will be there and I'm mixing Drum and Bass.'

I smile, 'yeah, we may come,' I say, 'where is it?'

'It's in an empty shop along Gloucester Road, next to the Free Shop,' James answers.

One of the girls with James joins in the conversation, 'I'm Jess, you should come and see what Bristol has to offer,' she smiles. 'Are you at university here?' Jess asks.

'Erm,' I stammer, not sure of what to say, 'no, I'm taking a sabbatical. I'm a writer.' I've inadvertently revealed a true ambition of mine to justify my reasons for being in Bristol. I feel suddenly like I've returned to *normal* society, and I feel self-conscious.

'Cool, there'll be plenty of life at the party for you to experience,' Jess states and starts to inflate a balloon with a silver canister and then sucks the balloon until it deflates. 'Would you like one?' she questions. Their fun attitude gives me some light relief from my anxieties and trauma.

'Okay,' I say. Jess offers one to me and Innit. We suck all the gas in until the balloons deflate. Suddenly I feel lightheaded, as if I've taken visual space-dust, the world sparkles.   'Anyway, we have to go, come tomorrow night to the party.'' Jess advises. She is cool in her ripped and laddered tights and boots, looking Spanish with her dark hair and olive skin.

'Yes, hope I see you,' James adds, I notice Innit has gone quiet. Jess seems nice. Innit and I watch them leave. Jess has picked up all the silver canisters, which look like chucky bullets, and disposes of them nearby.

'You... pretending that you're a writer, you almost had me believing you,' Innit smirks, 'so you aren't homeless then, in it.'

'Innit, you're just jealous,' I say, picturing Jame's green eyes in my mind and seeing his nice cheekbones. He has a handsome and pretty face. This is a weird enigma. Innit is good looking too in a different sort of way. I'm not interested in becoming entangled with anyone for a long time; I don't feel ready because of what's happened

We lay back on the green.

'Sara,' Innit says, 'I know you don't want to talk about your partner, where's your family?

'In Camberley, Surry, they moved recently,' I explain.

'Couldn't you return home,' Innit asks in earnest.

I reply, 'no, it's just my mum and she wouldn't want me there.'

We fall asleep and when we awake the light is fading.

Chapter Three; The Stars at Night

Innit and I go to find Squirrel. We take our time, ambling down the road towards the bus station and veering left, approaching the entrance of Cabot Circus. We cross over the busy road and pass interesting shops. Innit takes me on a miniature tour inside this shopping centre, we go down two sets of escalators and out the entrance at the bottom. We are now in the main shopping walkway and go back out, left, bearing right, passing the white sails and cables of the artistic structure, and along a street covered in graffiti.

We turn in by boards of abstract multi-coloured paintings and pass a sign saying 'police', which ironically has graffiti all around it. We pass a riot-van and come out the end of another busy road. I see a five-pointed large, colourful design on a building. Across from us is a bronze statue of a monk riding a horse with no bridle or saddle, in the centre of a circular cobbled area, he looks in frankness at me, showing his bare knees beneath his sackcloth clothes. And we approach a mediaeval house with wooden beams on the outside and low ceilings, which has been converted into a fish and chip shop, and up the many steps with a sign saying

'Christmas Steps', these have been worn down over the years, carrying on uphill past an old bookstore and hairdressers.

We are across from the hospital which has a big metal artwork of a few coloured rings attached to curving metal poles. There are two men dressed in blue with two empty wheelchairs standing in front of the sign, saying 'Bristol Royal Infirmary', they're wheeling the invisible men. As we cross over and stand by a coffee van, I can smell the cakes and feel hungry. We pass rows of bikes and hear the constant drone of traffic, now stopping at the red lights. We turn, passing a Georgian square with people sitting on benches in a green encircled with trees.

I see a sign saying Jamaica Street which has loads of buildings with big graffiti pictures all over the front of them; one's painted entirely purple and has a big silver skeleton of a dinosaur on it. People pass us on bicycles. We go by a shop saying 'Street Art Shop' which is across from the triangular green, nicknamed Turbo Island according to Innit, and Squirrel's where we left him, still looking dejected as he irritates people by asking them for their money.

Squirrel's whole face changes when he sees us, this reminds me of the symbolic theatre masks, comedy and tragedy. A smartly dressed woman is nearby and looks at us disdainfully.

'I just got a twenty-pound drop,' he updates us, smiling like a Cheshire cat, and rises to his feet. 'Let's go, come on,' he says.

The light is starting to fade into early evening, soon to become night. Streetlamps are already on as we run down the road laughing. I'm accepted. I feel better. We stroll along, taking in our urban environment, and come to another square green surrounded by tall black railings.

Across the road is what appears to be a church but has a sign saying 'Circlomedia' hanging above an arched entrance. The top of the tall steeple is lit up red, then purple and blue in succession, making the place look interesting.

'Is that a church?' I ask Squirrel.

'It used to be, it's a circus school now,' he answers. 'This is Portland Square where all the working-girls hang out,' Squirrel enlightens me.

'What?' I ask, not quite understanding.

'Working-girls, sex-workers, you know....'he answers with a bemused look on his face, I could tell he was slightly suspicious of me because of my question.

'I know what you mean, sorry,' I reply, 'it's just that I didn't know they had a circus school here that is incredibly cool.'

Squirrel smiles, 'yeah, you can learn juggling, acrobatics, stilt walking and aerial hoop. I knew a girl who went there, she was really good.'

Squirrel has relaxed again with me, he's a great alternative tour guide. The incite he has into Bristol's seedier side could be of use. This square used to be the centre for the slave trade in Bristol, it has a weird feeling about it; maybe the ghosts of the past haunt this place, or, maybe places tarnished by evil are prone to this returning and have an altered energy that needs healing, or, maybe it just looks a bit drab and at night this can make the place seem scary, especially from my viewpoint of being in a strange place with strangers. All the Georgian buildings in this square have big front-doors and many floors with high ceilings, the servants would live in the small poky attic.

Then I noticed two women in short skirts and low-cut tops standing around this green. One woman has tights on, but these were snagged up with dried blood and bruises beneath the snags. The women kept moving around to combat the boredom by shifting from side to side, or doing half spins, as they watched intently for their source of income to drive by.

Squirrel stops. 'I've just got to talk to Rene for a minute. I promised I'd look after her tonight. She's a *working-girl* if you haven't guessed.' He motions to the young woman with the snagged tights. Her clothes are meant to be tight but are hanging off her and her skirt is short, this just covers her non-existent ass, and her thick afro hair is held off her face with a hair band. She looks like a stick insect.

'How were you going to look after her?' I ask.

'I get paid to stand around and note down the punters' number plates just in case,' he answers. 'I've just got to make sure Rene has someone to do this for her tonight.' He makes his way over to her and I follow. As I get closer, I notice that Rene has cheap black slip-on shoes with shiny sequins on the front that are flaking off in places.

Squirrel starts to converse with Rene. 'Alright Rene, this is Sara. She's just come to Bristol and doesn't know anyone. Are you okay if I don't do the usual tonight? I need to show her the ropes.'

Rene looks a bit annoyed. She gets out her mobile and rings a friend and asks them to come and fill in for Squirrel promising *to sort them out*, as she phrases it. Rene is my age, you can tell by her manner and clothes, but her face looks worn out probably from lack of sleep. She could be very pretty if she put on a bit of weight and had some rest. I want to ask why she has bruises and blood on her skin, but I didn't know her well enough.

'What are you staring at?' She asks me curtly.

'Oh sorry, I was just noticing that you need some new tights. I've got some in my bag,' I say, as she looks me up and down. I get them out and hand them to her. They are just plain black tights, but they are without holes. Rene smiles at me and rolls down her old ones and throws them over the railings.

'I'm going to score now, come on Sara,' Squirrel announces. He is starting to count out his change including two and one pences.

'While you are scoring, I'll stay here and look after Rene until her friend arrives,' I say. This will give us a chance to become acquainted.

'Make sure you note down the number plates of the car I get into next,' Rene instructs and hands me a pencil and small notepad.

Squirrel saunters off and Innit stays with me. I watch as Rene waves to me and gets into a white ford escort van. I write out the letters and numbers. It sickens me to see her go off.

Really, we should have stopped her and thrown something at the man's car; she could come back beaten up or worse, she mightn't even come back. Rene is putting her life in danger. Innit and I just wait there on the curb.

Rene did come back this time, she calls out, 'he's one of my clients. If it's a stranger, I'll do a secret wave.'

Her feet touch the pavement and another car comes crawling around. Rene is off again into another silver Golf. She waves to me secretly as she gets in and takes her time so I can note the full number plate down and vehicle manufacturer. I wonder how much she makes. Innit informs me that this is Brunswick Square. He points out the Bristol Drug Project, this is where he goes to get clean syringes at the Needle Exchange.

Innit starts to express his annoyance about an experience he had there earlier, 'those drug counsellors take their time, they are trying to get me to go in for a one to one counselling session, for fuck sake, in it. They were asking me questions about whether I'd like acupuncture. I was like, no,' he says in an exaggerated voice, 'the only needles I want today are clean syringes so I can intravenously inject heroin and crack, der, I'm a drug addict, fucking treat me as such, in it.'

I laugh, it wasn't funny; I laugh when I'm nervous. I realise that I'm becoming desensitised to the seriousness of the situation; I'm in the company of two homeless drug addicts. Squirrel returns twenty minutes later with a bottle of cider and we go and sit on the green, walking through one of the arched gateways, onto the path, and into the middle grass covered area. All three of us wait for Rene to reappear so we can say goodbye. I pulled the blades of grass up and sprinkled them onto the ground, noticing the dry brown patches. Evening is drawing in.

'Where the fuck is she, in it?' Innit is getting annoyed. Rene resurfaces.

'Yo, yo,yo,' Rene pops out of the silver car. She must spend her life getting in and out of cars and not going anywhere except into a secluded car park or turn off. 'You lot are fine to go, Mickey is here now.'

Squirrel and Innit wave to a male coming towards us. We leave Rene. Squirrel stomps along in front of us with Innit and I following.

I call out to Squirrel, 'where are we going?'

'To a park,' he answers. 'We're going to have a smoke, a drink, and then sleep; how does that sound?'

'Okay,' I answer, funnily enough I do like Squirrel's and Innit's company, even though they use drugs and have nowhere to live, they are like no one I've ever met before.

We march up past the park and onto a main road. After a twenty-minute brisk walk along nameless roads, we come to our sanctuary in the park. Innit has already been in a newsagents to buy his necessities: foil, citric acid (for tenderising meat, or cooking up heroin, according to Innit, only available in Indian newsagents), cigarettes, a cheap lighter, as well as a pop bottle and chewing gum for making a pipe along with one of Innit's clean syringe (the head cut off with Squirrels penknife to create a downpipe to suck out the smoke from the pop bottle).

We sit around the improvised table and get high. I smoke heroin for the second time. I promise myself I'll never do this again. I just want to feel included and feel that nice numb feeling I felt before, I need to squish some of my uneasiness. We sit silently. I am sitting up and my head is between my legs and resting on the floor. I 've no worries, nothing matters, and my partner's death goes out of my thoughts. I only get up to projectile vomit over in a bush and then sit straight back down. Innit's dribbling with his head resting against the table. I'm wearing my metaphorical pink-tinted sunglasses, that's better, they provide unassailable protection.

After an hour, I start to come around. It's dark. My vision keeps going blurry and it takes me a while to be able to talk without slurring my words. I feel amazing, out of this world, covered in a ball of thick warm fur.

Innit laughs at me, 'are you okay?' he asks, 'come on let's get some sleep, in it.'

Innit lies down and so do I. I feel exhausted. I try to reply but keep forgetting what I'm saying in mid-sentence. We lie down together, sharing my unzipped sleeping bag, and Innit covers us with a blanket over the top of this. I'm so relaxed... relaxed. I'm with my new best friends, as comfortable as if I'm in my bed with my deluxe, memory foam, pink mattress, and pink duck-feather cushions and duvet. I have a soft pink cotton sheet. Innit puts his arm around me to keep warm...warm.

I fall asleep listening to the sound of Innit's breathing and the leaves rustling. I can see the hazy pink stars through the out-of-focus branches, and they are shining like pinhole sized pink spotlights in space, sparkling like stunning diamonds. I remember the quote by Oscar Wild, 'We are all in the gutter but some of us look up to the stars,' how fitting this is now. I can remember my mother saying she hoped all my dreams would come true.

Nightmare One; The Reinterpreted Fairy-Tale 'The Red Shoes', by Hans Christian Andersen (1845).

Suddenly, I find myself roaming in the field near my family home. I have on pink-tinted sunglasses and the vast expanse of the sky is bright pink above me. I'm happy. Nothing in the world appeals more to me than the sunglasses. I believe, with my sunglasses on, I can transform and become beautiful; like the ugly duckling became the beautiful swan in the fairy-tale. I know I'm not ugly, but sometimes I feel inadequate.

I start to dance up the garden path to my house. My mum opens the front door. The door, which I knew to be yellow, looks orange when mixed with pink. I dance in front of her to the music in my mind.

I hear my mother's voice; 'Sara what are you doing? Take off those sunglasses and stand still for a minute,' she commands, 'I need you to help me today.'

But I carry on dancing through the field beside my house. I hear the different bird calls and feel the warmth of the sun on my skin. The countryside melts into the front garden of the house I stayed in with my partner as I dance on towards him. All I can think about is how good I look in my pink-tinted sunglasses. I dance around him until I feel dizzy.

He asks, 'Sara, I haven't seen you for a while, where have you been? Please stand still and take off those sunglasses.' He looks frustrated.

He unsuccessfully tries to grab me as I dance, I pull away from his grasp and he glares at me in exasperation. I continue along the road, passing houses, until his calling voice becomes inaudible against the London traffic. The road suddenly changes, and I'm now dancing up the busy Gloucester Road in Bristol; the Graffiti is more vibrant than usual when mixed with the pink tint of each lens of my fantastic glasses. I watch everyone around me as I dance past newsagents and food stores. Then I turn down the road and up the steep slope leading to a house, but by this time I'm feeling remorseful for ignoring my family. I dance through the gate and up the garden path. The front door is open.

I dance up the stairs, into a bedroom, and see Innit on the floor. A blue mask that covers all your face and around the back of your head, with neon-pink and blue wool for hair, is placed on the floor next to Innit. The eye holes show the inside, which isn't painted, and newspaper print shows through. At a glance, the mask can be mistaken for someone's head sticking out of the floor. The shape is realistic, with moulded ears, nose and cheekbones. I had made an identical one for my costume in a school play. Then I dance into another room and find this to be empty, so I go back to see Innit.

As I dance, I realise that Innit is motionless; I can't tell if he is breathing. I manage to stay still and try to reach down for his wrist to feel for a pulse. Then the glasses transform from pink to pitch black and I can no longer see. I've suffered a blackout. I grab at the sunglasses, trying to tear them off, scratching my face in the process; they seem to be moulded on. I tug and attempt to pull them off. The glasses seem to be sculpted to my face and are stuck fast.

I feel for Innit's figure in the void and instead of being warm he is freezing cold and rigid. I scream, stumbling around and praying to God for help but he doesn't respond; maybe the fact that I'm praying is enough. My hands feel around on the floorboards and come across a sharp knife. I reach for the handle and place the blade on my neck, starting to hack away at my skin. Soon, my head is just attached by a thin flap of skin. I identify being like the thumb stump in the Sylvia Plath poem, 'Cut'.

Then, as it falls to the floor, someone switches my head with the papier-mâché mask. I stroke my wool hair. I explore inside the holes of my eye sockets. Where Is My Mind? Suddenly the mask is lifted back off my head, someone replaces this with my real head and the skin grows and connects to my neck, sunglasses removed, and I turn to see my partner hurling the mask away like a beach ball. This disintegrates into sand as it hits the ground; with grains that, when magnified, are all individual shapes, like snowflakes, an assortment of colour and perfect.

I'm now on the beach portrayed in the magazine I read in Doctor Hansel's surgery. My partner is with me. I feel his presence. I look out at the sea, feeling a deep sense of relief, and then I see Innit being taken away in a houseboat. I saw this boat in the park today. A strange figure in a dark sweatshirt, with the hood up obscuring their face, is beside him. The waves are almost engulfing the boat as it gets further and further away. The boat sinks. I start to cry, waking to Innit shaking me. I'm trembling. I'm lucky to have awoken unscathed but covered in dirt and leaves. Innit has pulled all the sleeping bag over him whilst asleep, leaving me wrapped only in the scratchy blanket which has left a red rash on my skin.

Chapter Four; The Awakening in Bristol

I dream about my dead partner and wake up trembling and crying. As I said before, I'm lucky to have awoken unscathed. I hear the birds chirping at first light. It's as if the world can't decide whether to be night or day. I wipe away the sleepy dust from my eyes and notice something in my peripheral vision; there's a magpie up on one of the branches, the grey beak looks like granite, Its black eyes are almost indistinguishable from the head feathers, the magpie's long tail-feathers splay out and the grey clawed-feet grip the branch to support its weight, the feathers shimmer an iridescent blue on the magpie's back.

As I gaze up at the bird, I remember that the Cuckoo lays their eggs in another bird's nest and, when hatched, the chicks evict the other birds' smaller chicks. We are all at the bottom of the tree as if we've been kicked out of our nest. One magpie is for sorrow, I say good morning to it whilst willing another magpie to appear. The magpie has probably been attracted to the silver foil left scrunched up on the ground, drugs paraphernalia is scattered all around the two other sleeping bodies, I get up and chuck this in a carrier bag and watch the bird take flight. My favourite bird is the robin because their sense of direction is amazingly accurate.

Innit has left a dirty needle out with the lid off, he must have done more stuff when I was asleep, I put this in his Sin-Bin, which rattles like a pencil case; I'm trying to link the alien things around me to a normal object to calm myself. I want a home. The sight of the syringe has unsettled me. As if by magic, another Magpie flies onto a branch near the first; two is for joy. I feel slightly better.

'Morning, in it,' Innit almost whispers and looks around him. 'What's wrong, Sara?' Innit asks, looking concerned.

He gives me a hug and I try to dispel the feeling of loss my nightmare has generated. Innit stretches, then sneezes and wretches, he doesn't look full of the joys of life with tears streaming down his face.

'I'm just going for a piss, in it,' he states and goes behind a bush some distance away. I hear him puke up. He comes back shivering and gets inside his sleeping bag again. 'I just have to *cook up* my morning *hit*, in it,' he explains.

He gets out a clean syringe ready, I force myself to watch. If I want to be a writer, then I need to be able to depict unpleasant situations; especially if I want to be a journalist ...oh for the life of the rich and famous, I would love to be famous for being truly talented in a way which would lift the universal consciousness and enrich humanity with insight or to create universal enjoyment. That would then bring wealth which would then be used to fund charity and creative, or worthwhile endeavours, with the health of the planet in mind; how cool would that be? 'People say I'm a dreamer, but I'm not the only one', the song by John Lennon plays in my mind.

Innit cautiously empties the heroin into his spoon with a pinch of citric acid which appears like salt. He draws up some clean water and sprays this onto this mixture. He holds a lighter flame under the spoon until the brown powder has dissolved into a clear liquid. He then takes a piece of filter from a cigarette and drops this in the liquid. He places the needle on this filter and pulls the plunger back, drawing the whole lot up into the syringe. Innit starts pumping up his arm. When satisfied that he can get a vein, he jabs the pin into the bulging vein and pulls back, until blood appears, and then pushes the thing all the way down so the liquid disappears into his arm. The evidence that he uses himself as a pin cushion is covering his skin. I sit watching, morbidly fascinated.

'Why do you do that to yourself?' I ask. 'Use a syringe I mean?'

'I'm an addict, in it. It's the best buzz, in it. Anyway, what else is there to do in this shit life?' Innit looks at me sincerely.

He's stopped shaking now and is starting to roll his green sleeping bag up. The sky appears beautiful this morning. The world holds such beauty and such ugliness. I feel to be ecstatically happy you need to have experienced extreme sadness; otherwise how else would you know? And the one way to qualify the depth of these emotions is through the expression of feelings in others, like music. Some popular music sickens me by trivialising human feelings, and experiences, my friend would say this is music for children or the incredibly simple, this would worry me because maybe by simplifying things we are keeping things light-hearted, maybe feeling too much is dangerous, the love for my partner is deep and I feel such sadness, if I had less capacity to feel love, then maybe I would be happier, or, maybe it would diminish all meaning and we would become Spice robots.

Innit couldn't really think that there is nothing else to do in life, how sad is that? Doctor Hansel would always advise me that there's so much good stuff to do, surfing, going to visit places like the Seven Wonders of the World, learning cosmology, philosophy, theology, English literature and the forms of criticism, history, art, classical and conceptual. The capacity for human beings to feel and express their emotions in the arts and music, or to qualify their thoughts through subjects, or invent things for the good of humanity, is amazing, anything other than dwelling in a depressive state, or, in Innit's case, sticking a needle in his arm. Yet, there was something appealing about this to me, maybe subconsciously I have a death wish.

The song by Placebo comes to mind, these words seem apt for Innit and my situation, 'in the shape of things to come, too much poison come undone, because there is nothing else to do, every me and every you' (good words). All I can compare how I am feeling is to a holey boat on the river; if I don't keep bailing the water out, the boat will sink, this is a burden and can leave me worn out and with the anxiety that at some point I might not have the strength to bail out the water, or fall asleep for too long, and then I will sink into the murky river water and never been seen again. Doctor Hansel had prescribed me anti-depressants, but they had just kept me awake for three days so I stopped taking them. Doctor Hansel would say that life is a gift.

Early morning always seems bright and untarnished. Very few people are around. As we wander to the newsagents, the occasional car or person passes us in a hurry to get to work. Bristol's rife with quirky graffiti and this makes the walk interesting. Innit has a cigarette as we wait five minutes for the shop to open.

'Come then, in it,' Innit announces when the shop door is unlocked, and we go to get some food. The Indian shopkeeper watches us, this makes me feel awkward. I stroll down the aisles trying to find something that I feel like eating, Innit does the same. I scan all the confectionery in front of the till. I decide on some manky looking bananas, a carton of cranberry juice and some LA tanned croissants.

We stroll back to the park, climbing through the misshapen hole in the fence again. When we are back, Innit unzips his coat and numerous things fall out of the arms, he's stolen loads of stuff, this alarms me.

'Innit, don't ever do that with me again. I 've got to keep a low profile.'

'Are you running from the police, in it?' he asks.

'Yeah, in a way, keep that to yourself,' I reply, really, I just don't want to get in trouble.

We go through the bushes to our little den. I nudge Squirrel gently till his bleary eyes open and pass around the bananas and croissants and we eat our breakfast. Afterwards, we pack the blankets up and hide them in a black bag behind some bushes and wander into the centre.

'Thanks for looking after me last night,' I declare in earnest, pulling my plaited hair back in a ponytail, the small plaits are starting to itch.

'You're our friend and we're going to look after you until we know you are okay,' Squirrel answers. 'You can't sleep outside on your own.'

'What are we going to do today?' I enquire.

'Well, as it happens, I get my sick money off the DHSS today,' Squirrel announces enthusiastically. 'I always feel like it's my birthday on paydays. I'm going to take this out at the Post Office in the Galleries, then I reckon we should go and sit in Castle Park and have a drink.'

'What's the Galleries?' I ask.

Innit answers, 'another shopping precinct, in it, I showed you Cabot Circus yesterday just down from there.' Innit then turns to Squirrel and says, 'there's a party tonight, we met some people in the park yesterday and they said about it, in it. It's going to be held in one of the empty shops on Gloucester Road, next to the Free Shop, in it.'

'Cool, it sounds like we're going to have a good time tonight then,' Squirrel responds, 'it's better than sleeping out on the streets, we can kip in the shop, we might be able to squat the place after.'

We wander through Portland Square and I look at the Georgian architecture, some of the buildings are boarded up and empty, they're falling into disrepair. Then we pass the glass office building and wait in the middle of the Pelican Crossing. The road's busy here. We saunter past McDonald's and go through the slipway out into the central shopping area. We go left and along the paved area, with shops either side, there's a busker playing guitar and a woman handing out pieces of cinnamon pretzels. Squirrel and Innit take a piece each and shove it in their mouths, you could say they were building up their natural immune system.

As we walk on, we see the sails of white canvas sheltering the chairs and tables in front of the hot dog stand at the end of the road, bus drivers in blue are sitting there with their morning coffees. We pass a group of homeless people sitting in a doorway and they all look stupefied, they look like zombies with their eyes all glazed, one of them is dribbling. Innit and Squirrel nod hello to the ones that notice and are aware of them, some have their eyes shut and are leaning on each other.

'What's wrong with them?' I ask Innit.

'Spice...they are addicts, one drag can lead to a heart attack, people are dropping like flies, there is no substitute either so they can't get off it, in it,' Innit explains.

'I thought Spice was a legal high?' I ask.

'They made a big mistake with that, now the drug agencies have to deal with Spice addicts as well, in it, people will do anything to zombie out, time goes quicker then, in it.'

Squirrel adds, 'they don't have to think, forget all the trauma they have been through.' Squirrel stomps on up the road like a street soldier.

Chapter Five; The Spice Zombie

We pass a cafe with chairs outside and pass the rows of bikes and up to the left, going by Wilkinson and Waterstones until we reach the steps up to the glass door entrance. Innit sits on the steps. This must be the Galleries. We stand outside the entrance and wait for Squirrel to finish his roll up made of fag butts. A man peers over at both of us disdainfully; Innit has dirty jeans on, and creased, dirty clothes, his face is also a bit streaky, Innit looks like a homeless drug-addict basically, what you see is what you get with Innit, I realise that I probably look unwashed as well. Squirrel enters through the glass door, knocking his rucksack against the doorways, dreadlocks everywhere.

'Innit where can I freshen up?' I query.

'You say some weird things, 'Innit proclaims, 'If you mean you need a wash, then there is a toilet in The Galleries.'

'Good, I wish Squirrel would hurry up.'

We wait until his fag is done and then head in the entrance to the red brick building with a glass roof. We go through the glass doors and along past the shops and sweet stands, down the escalators in the open middle of the mall, then across to the toilets, past the lifts and the entrance to the carpark, trying not to get in people's way. I seem to be spending my life in public conveniences; I almost burst out laughing at the thought of my new frequencies.

I go past the full-length mirror, out the front of the Public Toilets, and blink at the artificial bright lights as I enter. The place is blue and white. The smell of toilet cleaner hits me, which smells quite fragrant, and reminds me of walking in a fern tree forest. I wash at the small basins with mirrors above them, finding this logistically difficult due to the water running while your hands are under the taps only, and do my make up as people go in and out of the cubicles provided, splashing water over my face with one hand and the tiled floor by accident. I get my black makeup bag out and do my eyeliner, mascara, I moisturise my face and put on some light foundation, I use some black eyeshadow to give definition to my eyes. I don't like looking in the mirror. Innit and Squirrel are waiting for me outside, both smiling and fooling around.

'You look nice, in it,' Innit says, 'are you okay?'

'Yeah,' I think so,' I answer, 'I feel unsettled Innit, I don't know where I am or where I'm going.'

Innit laughs, 'we are going to enjoy today and go to a party tonight, in it, come on, cheer up,' he smiles at me and puts his arm lightly around my neck.

We go back up the escalators until we are on the top floor of three and find the Post Office. We enter, Squirrel presses a button on the machine, gets a number, and sits in the seating area. His number lights up and he rushes to the relevant counter. He then turns towards us and fans out the money in his hand.

'That's for you Innit,' he explains and hands Innit a twenty-pound note. 'That's for you Sara,' he clarifies and hands me twenty pounds also.

I look at him, bemused, 'what's that for?' I ask.

'Just in case you need it, emergency funds, when you get some money you can pay me back.'

Squirrel doesn't get that much to live on, and he has nowhere to live, I can't believe his generosity.

'Thanks', I say.

We then wander up to Castle Park, passing mothers with babies in pushchairs and lads in baseball caps, and men and women in smart clothes and punks in jeans and leather jackets with bright Mohicans. A woman hands me a leaflet with a poem about love written on the front, and she informs me that this is from the scriptures; the polarisation of opinions, due to religious idealism and political orientation makes for an interesting world.

'I'm just going to go and get us a drink, wait for me on the green,' Squirrel states.

Innit and I walk past colourful flower beds and oak trees until we are on the green bank beside the river. We sit down, lie back and enjoy the morning sun, there is a slight chill in the air. I must have dozed off. Sleeping in parks is another regular occurrence and creates part of my new tailored routine.

I wake up, and Squirrel has returned with more cider.

'Cool Squirrel, in it,' Innit says and grins.

'It's a bit early for me,' I state.

'Come on, sweetheart,' Squirrel instructs, 'you're one of us now.'

I take the cider off him and gulp it back. It tastes horrible to start with, but I think I am growing accustomed to the taste.

'We're going to have a good day today,' Squirrel announces. 'And night, at the party on Gloucester Road.'

'Yeah,' Innit answers, 'see Bristol is a party city, there are *sick* parties all the time, Sara,' he affirms, 'you will be glad you came here; I promise. I have a good feeling about today, in it.'

The sun is shining, and I can feel the heat on my legs, making me sweat,and I roll my tight jeans up to my knees and look around me. Some people are sitting on the green and others walk or cycle past. It's still relatively early. I see a smart looking couple sipping their coffee on their way to work and start to feel homesick. I miss my early morning coffee in my reusable cup before I started my job, employment is no longer an option.

A trio of people approach us, a female and a male looking scruffy with a dog trailing beside them. The other male looks out of place because he's wearing smart sports stuff. The smarter one addresses Squirrel. He has a broad Bristolian accent.

'Squirrel, Innit, what go on?' the man asks. He's older than Innit.

They all stare at me, only the female half smiles.

'You okay, Kev,' Innit addresses the man I now know as Kev.

'Who this then?' Kev demands, his eyebrows knitting together.

'This is our friend and that's all you need to know, Bruv,' Squirrel answers.

'You touchy dickhead,' Kev replies disdainfully, he stands with his friends looking down on us, I shield my eyes to see.

'Kev, in it, this Sara, Sara this Kev, in it, and that Paula and Ferret, in it,' Innit says, to appease Kev. They all sit down next to us in a sort of circle. Kev sits next to Squirrel. 'Alright,' Paula says, addressing me to break through the tense atmosphere. I notice her hair is shaved down one side and she has big metal rings on her fingers, like knuckle dusters. 'I ain't seen you before,' she states, staring at me suspiciously.

I remember Innit's advice about not talking to anyone else apart from him and Squirrel and keep quiet. I feel intimidated by these new people. Kev gives me a weird look.

'Give us five-pound, Squirrel,' Kev demands, 'we want some drink.'

'Alright,' Squirrel says and fishes a fiver out of his pocket. Kev goes off, leaving scruffy Paula and Ferret with us. Squirrel appears to have lost his lustre for the day. I don't know these people, but I can tell they're not popular with Innit and Squirrel.

'Don't pay any attention to Kev, you know how he gets when he ain't got his Spice,' Paula counsels Squirrel.

Kev returns with some cans and sits down, passing Paula and Ferret one each.

'What up to today?' Kev probes.

'The usual,' Squirrel replies irritably.

'I smacked the shit out of this bloke last night, it was funny as fuck,' Kev announces proudly, 'we asked him for change and he ignored us so I punched him in the head and Ferret got his wallet off him.'

Innit and Squirrel remain silent.

'What's the matter,' Kev asks, 'we saw him being taken off in an ambulance, it was dark, he won't recognise us,' Kev smirks.

'Do you think that was really needed?' Squirrel asks, looking sad.

'He was some posh nonce who deserved it,' Kev replies. 'He's lucky I didn't stab him up.'

The capricious Chav Kev, sorry to use vernacular language, extracts his butterfly knife from his pocket, opens this, and starts to make slashing movements in the air. The silver blade shines. His face is contorted in a strange look of concentration. I stay completely quiet now, terrified. For a while, we all sit and finish our drinks. I try to ignore the new people. I feel mentally and physically disconnected from reality. Also, I haven't got my phone, I can't check my emails or look on WhatsApp or Messenger. I usually always have this ready to watch YouTube or check the news. Squirrel falls silent and I begin twiddling with my plaits.

'I think we need to move,' Squirrel advises, when all the alcohol has been exhausted. The white cider has gone to my head.

Kev faces Squirrel, 'what's the matter?' Kev declares with a mean look on his face, 'do you think you're too good for us or something you prick?'

Squirrel answers, trying to sound casual, 'don't be stupid, Bruv, we just have things to do that's all,' Squirrel starts dragging his rucksack towards him.

'You can give us money to get more drink,' Kev demands again, 'Squirrel, I know it's your Payday...' Kev is still playing with his knife.

'That's got nothing to do with you,' Squirrel asserts, looking irritated, 'I never ask you lot for jack shit.'

There is another unnerving silence and then Kev jumps up and kicks Squirrel in the side whilst I sit, frozen to the spot. Ferret and Paula's dog starts barking and Ferret grabs hold of the collar. Innit rises and faces Kev.

'Fuck off or I'll use this on you Innit.' Kev responds, scowling.

I scrambled to my feet. Kev's eyes have glazed over, he looks scary, like a ferocious animal.

'Go on then dickhead, in it,' Innit exclaims defiantly, and with that Innit lunges forward to get the knife off Kev.

Innit has seized the sharp end. Kev releases his grip on the handle. Ferret and Paula drag their dog away, the barking and growling is incessant, leaving Innit bleeding out of the laceration. Innit places the knife in his other hand and holds this up. I'm shaking.

'Fuck you, I'll have both of you, just you fucking wait,' Kev promises, almost growling like a rabid dog.

'You and whose army dickhead,' Squirrel yells. Kev looks from Innit to Squirrel, stares at the knife, and decides to follow his friends, yelling profanities as he goes.

I feel safer now, 'Innit let me look at your hand?' I ask. 'Are you going to report Kev,' it's weird saying his name.

Squirrel scoffs.

'The police won't help, I'm homeless, I don't want to get called a Grass,' Innit clarifies, looking deadly serious for a moment. 'Don't worry, in it,' Innit reassures me, 'it's only a flesh wound and could've been worse.'

I realise that if something happens to me, I won't be able to go to them either.

'That Kev's a nutter, we should have left immediately,' Squirrel declares. 'He's been smoking too much Spice.' This sentence is supposed to exonerate everything, at least The Devil isn't getting the blame this time.

''Keep pressure on the wound,' I advise, 'you both said today was going to be a good day,' I say and Squirrel and Innit burst out laughing.

Innit looks at his wound, 'this isn't as bad as I thought it would be, in it. I'm still alive, don't know if that is a good or bad thing,' he says, smiling.

Squirrel gets out a bottle of water from his rucksack and some tiny alcohol wipes and starts to clean Innit's hand. When this is done, he pulls out a roll of toilet paper and wraps it around the cut. I notice that Innit looks paler than usual, he has a pale complexion anyway, so he almost looks white, like an apparition.

Chapter Six; The Party

'We need to go via a shop and get you a bandage,' Squirrel advises. He has nursed the wound expertly; in another life he might have made a good paramedic.

As we go along to the shops, we chat about what just happened.

'Does that happen a lot?' I ask.

'Yes,' Innit replies. 'Being on the streets is a dangerous place.'

'We need to look after each other,' Squirrel replies, looking very serious. 'Living on the streets hardens you up to life, we need to be strong and have good survival skills, life will not always be this way, soon everyone will have to fight for survival and by then we will be the ones surviving in these extreme circumstances because we have trained for them.'

'Squirrel, not now, in it, please let's not talk about revolution right now,' Innit responds. 'We should try and find a squat to stay in, in it.'

'That sounds like a good idea, somewhere where Innit can rest and get better,' I reply, shaken by what has just happened.

'Let's go to this party tonight and see if the organisers have any ideas, if they found out about an empty shop then maybe they can find out about other places,' Squirrel suggests.

We stop in the Georgian Square, and Innit goes into the building through the bright pink door. I notice he is in pain. Squirrel and I wait, sitting on the bench in front. After a while Innit emerges with his hand bandaged expertly.

He smiles at us, 'the nurse gave me more bandages, in it. I've promised to check in with her next week, in it, 'I need to score now,' Innit declares, 'best pain killer in the world.'

'Okay,' Squirrel says, 'I'll go and get some stuff and we can go to the park,' Squirrel looks directly at Innit, 'you stay with Sara and wait for me. I don't want her with me, it will freak the dealers out, they might think she's police,' Squirrel grabs my hand and pulls me up from the bench. 'We can get cheap alcohol too from there,' he suggests.

We wander to the shops at the top of the Gloucester road and Squirrel runs in and gets him and Innit a can, I get a weaker larger, I can't drink strong lager, it's an acquired taste. Innit and I sit and drink this outside the shops waiting for Squirrel, I feel slightly apprehensive, I know I'm going to use heroin and crack again, I want to, I like the feeling this gives me. Squirrel returns in minutes and we go to use.

We sit in the park, near the children's play area and sit in the corner. We shield ourselves with our coats, so the lighter doesn't go out, and smoke pipes of crack cocaine and do lines of heroin on foil and Innit has *a hit* as he calls it, jabbing another needle into his veins. I am becoming accustomed to the sight. I feel amazing, warm, comfortable, and happy. I don't care what I look like, I don't care about anything. I have my pink-tinted sunglasses on which changes my perception of reality. My vision is hazy. Time passes and goes by unnoticed. I start to come back to earth after a while, hours have passed.

All three of us wander around, going into Bristol Drugs Project for free tea and coffee on Brunswick square. There is nothing much to do. Innit has his hand bandaged up and in a sling. We get more alcohol and sit out in the open by Castle Park. And we get food from sister Pauline and she is her happy, friendly self which cheers me up and makes me feel safer. Innit and Squirrel sit and chat to a few of their friends in the Bear Pit, whilst I sit quietly, only speaking when I'm being spoken to. I hear Kev's name being mentioned, connected to the lavish vocabulary 'cunt' and 'prick', as we sit on the grass bank. The sky is darkening. I start to feel uneasy.

'Sara, are you okay, in it?' Innit asks. He's sitting beside me.

'I'm scared,' I answer in a low voice so none of the people we are sitting with can hear, 'I can't believe you were stabbed, and you just see it as normal.'

'You get used to things like this happening when you live on the street,' Innit responds as the tears well up in my eyes.

Innit shuffles nearer to me and puts his arm around me, his dirty streaky sweatshirt smelling slightly. 'Don't be upset, we're going to that party soon,' he advises.

'Yes,' I reply, feeling better, I just want to be around some 'normal' people who don't swear, shout or drink heavily like Squirrel and Innit's friends.

'Anyway,' Innit answers, 'I can look after myself, don't worry. It ain't really hurting now anyway.'

Innit is brave. He had probably saved Squirrel from being hurt earlier and had risked his own life in the process. I can't believe the traumatic escapades some people have to go through every day.

The streetlamps have lit. More people are venturing around on their way to different locations, the city vibes are washing over me, and I can't help being excited. The cloak of night is mysterious and it's this which creates the feeling of exhilaration, yet, I still feel afraid and unhappy by today's events, and the longing for my partner which never goes away but can be obscured on occasions. Music is in the background, a busker sings and plays guitar in one of the tunnels, two policemen walk through this tunnel and the busker suddenly swaps the tune he is playing to the acoustic version of 'Borders' by M.I.A; 'Guns blow doors to the system, yeah fuck 'em when we say we're not with them', the policemen glance at each other nervously. I can see Squirrel talking on a mobile phone across from us under the streetlamp.

'Come on, we are going to see a man about a dog,' Squirrel announces illusively.

We're still sitting in a group on the verge. Innit rises and so do I, Squirrel is waiting for us. Then we march through the tunnel, past the singing man on the guitar and up the slope to the pavement on the other side, passing a giggling man in a hat, with teddy bear ears, strolling along with a female about my age in a fox outfit, with a mask pulled up on her head and a tail pinned to the back of her mini skirt. Passing another group of dressed up people, one is wearing a wrestler's outfit with gold shorts and big eighties sunglasses. Bristol is an eclectic place and seems to be full of funny people.

We mosey into the centre and come to a circle of white poles in between long backless benches which are supposed to look artistic I'm sure. The Galleries shopping centre entrance is in front of us. Someone is there waiting.

'Jay,' Squirrel calls and Jay waves. We approach a lad called Jay; he is dressed casually with long dark-brown-dreadlocked hair in a ponytail. Jay is around my age, twenty-three, and looks cool in a bright coloured tracksuit and baseball cap. He has a cute friendly face with big oval brown eyes. Squirrel sits on the bench beside him.

'I've just got here, Bruv,' Jay states and smiles, Innit and Jay make a fist each and touch them together, Innit uses his left hand.

We approach him and Squirrel sits on the bench beside him.

'Innit, I've heard you have been in the wars,' Jay says, peering at Innit's bad hand.

'It ain't nothing,' Innit states heroically. 'We're going to a party along Gloucester Road.'

'Oh, I've heard about that as well,' Jay responds, 'it should be *sick*.'

'Are you coming then, in it?' Innit asks.

'Later, I've got to drop tings off to someone first.' Jay reveals, 'I've that ting you want.' Jay surreptitiously passes Squirrel a small folded piece of paper. Jay looks at me and asks, 'who dis?'

'I forgot to introduce you, this is Sara, Bruv,' Squirrel responds, '

we're looking after her.'   'Is she safe,' Jay asks.

'Yeah, Sara's safe, in it.' Innit answers defensively, an absurd comment because really Innit hasn't known me for very long.

'Cool,' Jay replies, he touches fists with Innit and Squirrel. 'Anyway, laters, stay off the Spice, apparently people been dying, Fam. One of the Spice Heads was found dead with his cheek ripped off, we think it was a fox, Fam,' Jay proclaims and wanders off.

I look at Innit aghast. Innit links arms with me. The three of us meander up to Castle Park and sit by the water feature there, surrounded by bushes and sit down on the ground. It is nice here; we can hear the calming sound of the flowing water. Squirrel opens the rectangular wrap of paper which contains some powder. He tells me to have a dab with my finger. I do and shudder at the taste, Innit laughs.

'Give it here, in it,' Innit takes it from me, replicating my actions. 'Sara, we'll be *buzzing* soon, in it.'

'Let's stay here until we feel something off this stuff,' Squirrel advises.

After a while I notice that Innit's pupils have become massive, the complete opposite to what Innit's eyes usually look like. I'm starting to feel high, everything's becoming blurry. The lights have a star-like halo around them. I also feel strangely warm and when I breathe it feels like the world is breathing with me, like a sort of rush, I'm tingling. My skin feels all sensitive as I run my hand up and down the inside of my arm. There seems to be multicoloured dot patterns everywhere. I feel happy and full of energy. All I can think about is how good I feel in my metaphorical pink-tinted sunglasses.

'I said you would start buzzing, in it,' Innit states, smiling. 'Right, let's go and *DANCE*. Are you glad you met us then, Sara?'

'Yes,' I answer, feeling an inner contentment, 'If I hadn't met you and Squirrel who knows where I would be now.'

'I'm glad we met, Sara,' Squirrel discloses, 'I don't know why but I feel like we've known each other for ages.' Squirrel stands up and heaves his rucksack up over his shoulder as I have seen him do countless times, it's part of him.

We make our way down through the centre to the party. I feel like I'm floating. Innit links arms with me. I feel like he's the only reason why I don't float away. We roam up the Gloucester Road and there are numerous other people accompanying us; I don't know if the people are real or imaginary. The city lighting from all different sources, cars, shops, streetlights, enable us to find the way, the city is radiating, and we can hear the noise of chatting and music from the clubs and bars.

It isn't hard to locate the party; the crowd stood outside, and the loud music makes this elementary. The party's venue has a central doorway and big windows on either side. There are black curtains obscuring these windows so visibility inside is obscured. The people are all lined up waiting to enter, some are swaying about like they're inebriated. We wait in the line and eventually come to the doorway. The noise of the repetitive bass becomes more distinct the closer we get. Lights flash as the door opens like there is some magical world through them. I feel like Alice in Wonderland. I'm Alice. I drank the poison, the poison in fact has duality to it; toxic to some, a healing potion to others, like chasing White Rabbits.

As I go through the door, everything transforms in front of me. Suddenly I'm inside and colours glow. People are dressed in neon. I feel like I'm on an alien planet. I can sense the energy in this room and feel the body heat from the numerous people. There are big black sheets up on the walls with depictions of Celtic patterns and solar systems. The place is packed with people dancing. We make our way through the crowds, trying not to barge into anyone. It is hot here.

At the back of the shop, I catch a glimpse of James. I remember that he is DJing at this party. I move towards him and start to dance. Squirrel and Innit are beside me.

'Sara, we're gonna have a look around,' Squirrel declares loudly in my ear, 'stay here and we'll come back.'

I nod in response. I'm feeling slightly self-conscious, dancing with my small rucksack on. At least it isn't a big one like Squirrel's. As Squirrel strolls away, he's accidentally knocking people. I move nearer to the D.J and see Jess, from the park, in front of me. She's got glitter down one side of her cheek, and black eyeliner curling slightly at the corner of her eyes. She has fairy wings on and looks theatrical with a short skirt with netting underneath. I feel plainly dressed in comparison.

She sees me and waves, the music is blaring here. The speakers are piled up either side of the mixing desk which is positioned on a rectangular table covered in another black sheet. James is at a desk and is fiddling with buttons and spinning the decks, similar to record decks, as a new beat starts to play over the existing music. When I go over to Jess, she hugs me. Jess pulls me behind the stack of speakers where it's slightly quieter.

'You came then, Cinderella shall go to the ball with her fairy godmother Jess,' Jess proclaims, smiling, 'come on, we can go and say hello to James.'

Jess takes my hand and goes over to James who's going through his music library on his memory stick pulling up the next few tunes. Jess pokes James and he turns around and she ushers him over to talk. We go back behind the speakers. He mixes in a couple of tunes and then comes over to join us for a minute. James has a silver hood tied around his neck with springs with eyes attached to them like bee antennas. He takes off the hood and ties this round my neck, pulling the hood up over my plaited hair. I smile. That's a relief.

I feel like James is psychic, like we're all part of a universal consciousness and are trying to help one another. I don't have to speak because everyone knows what I need, I don't have to say anything, I can feel the bass going through me and resonating within my very soul almost. This is the best party I've ever been to.

He smiles, 'hello Sara, good to see you,' he shouts over the music, 'I'll be finished soon and I'll come and talk to you, put your bag behind here,' he grabs this off my back and goes back to mix music, hiding my bag under the table with the record decks on.

Jess and I carry on dancing, the music is too loud to do anything else. I feel like I'm part of the music. People keep joining me and we dance together harmoniously, smiling. I feel happy. Hand in hand with Jess again, she leads me off the dance floor. I pull my hood down. We go to relax on a sofa positioned under a stairwell, I take off James's hood because the springs stick in my back. Above us, people are sitting on the steps and chatting. A guy comes and sits beside me, Jess is on one side and this man on the other.

He looks at me and says, 'don't worry about me, the doctor reckons that I've fried the nerve endings in my brain through taking too much ecstasy.'

'Okay,' I reply in an uncertain tone, I don't know what else to say.

As I'm chatting with Jess, I hear this man talking to himself, so I listen to him, and Jess, and throw in the odd word into his conversation so it doesn't look like he is talking to himself; essentially I'm having two conversations at once and Jess is oblivious. The man gets up and wanders off dancing, he seems quite happy; just mentally challenged.

I spot Innit and Squirrel, they're over the other side of the room. I shout and wave to get their attention over the murmur of voices and loud continuous baseline. They join us, pulling over some chairs to do so. Squirrel must have placed his bag somewhere.

'Are you enjoying yourself?' I ask.

'Yeah, it's a banging party,' Squirrel answers.

'Hello,' Innit addresses Jess, 'I met you in the park, your name's Jess, in it?'

'Yes, and you're Innit,' Jess replies. Innit tries to get something out of his pocket with his left hand and drops his tobacco on the floor. Jess notices the bandages on his other hand, 'what happened?' she asks and picks up his tobacco from under his chair.

'Oh...erm...well we met an idiot in the park who wanted to have a go for no reason, in it,' Innit answers awkwardly.

James appears from out of the dancing crowd, 'hi,' he says, and perches on the end of the sofa next to me. I move to let him sit down, turn to him and smile. I still feel all tingly.

Innit carries on his conversation with Jess, 'when you sleep *out* you have to put up with this sort of thing, it comes with the territory,' he declares with an air of resignation.

'What's this?' James asks. 'Haven't you lot got anywhere to live then?'

'No,' Squirrel states, 'we met Sara at the bus station and have been looking after her ever since.'

'I know of an empty property on the way up to ours, I will jot down the address for you, it's on Richmond Road, five minutes from here, in Montpelier, apparently the house has been empty for ages,' James reveals, looking cool in his green and blue Adidas T-shirt.

Squirrel replies, 'yeah that sounds like a good idea, it's weird, because we came here to see if anyone knew of any places we could squat. Good, Sara has been unsettled due to what happened today,' Squirrel says in response.

'I'm not surprised,' Jess adds.

'If this works out, hopefully we'll all be safer,' Squirrel states, smiling at me as he hands James a pencil to write the house number down on a flyer Squirrel has. James hands the flyer back with the all-important address.

A shadow comes towards us, framed by the flashing lights. As it gets closer, I see the dreadlocked ponytail and realise it's Jay.

'I've got a treat for us,' he explains, tipping some powder onto the fleshy bit in between my thumb and fingers.

He then tips some onto his hand and does the same. I feel compelled to take the stuff, really, I should be strong enough to say no, I already feel strangely euphoric and not in control. I have my pink-tinted sunglasses on. Jess and James refuse the stuff. I wonder what impression I'm making. The stuff is making me feel happier and is blocking out my trauma. I remember my partner, but the thought is fleeting because of the substances I've taken. I would be reminded again though. This would only be a short-term release from the despair I feel. Drugs are not the answer, I need proper support and counselling to be able to cope with my trauma. I don't get this.

We dance for ages; everything seems bright and blurry. After a while I start to feel thirsty. 'I need to get some water,' I say, going right up close to Innit so he can hear me.

'Follow me,' Innit states and goes up to a stall right at the back of the shop.

'Give us a bottle, in it,' Innit orders the person behind this.

He hands him a bottle. I start to feel light-headed and faint. Innit gives me a supporting hand.

'Let's go outside and get you some fresh air, in it,' Innit says and puts his arm around my waist.

We make our way as quickly as possible through to the front door and out onto the pavement and I throw up. Innit holds my plaited hair back out of my face. People are staring at me.

'Is she okay,' a girl asks.

'Yes, I'm looking after her, in it,' Innit replies. He turns back to me and says, 'I reckon we should go and get Squirrel and we could go find our new house.'

'Yes,' I say as I take a drink of water, I am feeling better.

Innit goes back inside the party to get Squirrel, as I lean shivering against the wall. My vision keeps going blurry. As he opens the door, I hear music getting louder and then become muffled again as the door closes. I think about my partner and feel upset. I try to push all these thoughts to the back of my mind. Squirrel emerges.

'I was getting bored of the party anyway,' Squirrel states.

Innit, Squirrel and I stroll through the streets to get to the squat, stopping at the twenty four-hour shop with people outside. This place is dubious at this time and I'm glad my friends are with me; shadowy people hang around as if they are about to jump out on you. Gloucester road is nosey and busy, the clubs and bars are open with people outside either waiting to get in or getting air, with pint glasses in hand. I'm glad there are 'normal' people around, not just the scavengers. Innit touches fists with a few of them as they pester people for money.

Squirrel says, 'go in that twenty-four shop and get some cans of lager. Get us a four pack to share, we deserve a drink, be quick Sara, you have enough money ain't you.'

'Yes,' I answer, I'd hardly spent anything since being here.

'I'll come with you, in it,' Innit adds.

Innit's going to get his discount. I leave him to this. I stroll around the busy shop which now has a pink tint, there is a man out of his head sat on the crates of larger, I smile at him. I recognise the pink tinged gold cans that I have seen Squirrel gulping back and reach for two four packs of the chilled extra strong lager. I'll have to drink strong lager because I can't be bothered to mess around and Squirrel wants me to be swift. Innit has already left and is outside. I wonder what his has managed to tax; street tax, the same thing as the government tax, except we can get in trouble for it, law enforcement has CS gas, some have guns, but this is rare, luckily this is not America, oh, and obviously we don't pay for schools, doctors, dentists and the NHS eherm.

We amble past the bar and further up to where the drunks sit. And, by The Art House café, with its leather sofas and walls full of art, we stop at a set of traffic lights and Innit ushers me across the busy dual carriage road. We cross over and turn right, to the left, behind us now, is a huge painting on a wall saying boycott Tesco, with blue writing on a pink background, I wonder why, and the high-rise council blocks which are like rabbit hutches. We are now going past the Salvation Army shop and long wooden boards full of graffiti are across the road. On the corner, as we enter Picton Street, trees grow out of paving grills.

As we turn, a shadowy corrugated iron building meets my eyes with more graffiti which is hard to see in the dark, and mixed with pink, I would look in the daytime. I pull my hood up over my head. On our side, numerous coloured posters are stuck up on metal doors on the corner advertising various club nights, they are stuck over the top of other posters and some are ripped, the door looks like a collage.

We all start to make our way along the road and turn left, down the hill and past some shops, on the large paving area which stretches between the local businesses, creating a walkway, and turn right up the steep suburban street past three-small-metal-skips. The corner shop has graffiti all over the blinds; in the dark I can still see that tags are everywhere, on the walls, and even road signs. The paved area has a big wooden planked barrel and two half barrels with plants inside, these are tagged along with the skips. I can't make out the words. And up the narrow steep road with cars either side. I wouldn't be able to cycle up this steep road without practice and perseverance.

We pass an archway with an abandoned armchair connecting to the adjacent road, and stop opposite a pub. I smell bonfires. Someone's footsteps are coming towards me, a woman in a hooded cardigan, with teddy bear ears on, is walking on the other side of the road. Leaves rustled in the breeze, accompanied by the high whizzing of bicycle wheels as a man sped past me; making me jump. Strands of my hair, which have become free from the plates, tickle my face and nose. I pull my hood up.

Then uphill past the pub, but it's hard to really see because it's still dark, and my vision is still blurry and pink. We carry on until we come to the house. Innit goes across the open garden-path and we stand in front and go up to the front door. I stand back surveying the place, with its front bay windows and brick, the sandy colour of Bath stone. These two floored houses look Victorian and will have the coving and large skirting that are advertised as original features in the windows of estate agents. There is a small front garden and a gated path leading up to the orange door.

Squirrel looks through the window in the front door and knocks, 'this is the house, I'm going to see if I can get around the back.'

'Be careful,' I say, genuinely apprehensive.

Innit and I stand in the garden waiting, and then sit on the garden wall. Innit has put on his sweatshirt with the hood up, we are both incognito.

'I hope no one is living here, I can imagine Squirrel running past being chased by the owner, in it,' he says.

Squirrel then opens the door with a big smile on his face, 'come inside,' he says.

I wander up to the door and instantly Squirrel reaches for my carrier bag. He can smell larger and has the nose of a sniffer dog; I can imagine Squirrel as a mongrel, a collie crossed with a greyhound, slightly mixed up but intelligent.

'Welcome to our humble abode,' Squirrel announces as if we have just won the lottery. He has lit up T-candles in the hallway. I enter the shadowy corridor. Innit tries the light switches. The corridor is bare, no pictures and no carpet; just wooden floorboards with the carpet tacking around the edge of the walls still in place.

Innit empties out his hoodie arms and has got some food and a couple of light bulbs, 'I need to go and investigate, find the electric meter so I can wire it up, you have some cable Squirrel?'

Squirrel takes out the cable and hands this to Innit. Innit is off, looking round in every nook and granny whilst Squirrel and myself sit waiting in the lounge. This room has furniture, a carpet, two big sofas, shelves, and a coffee table. He returns.

'Sara, take the candle; I need to put in the bulb in the front room. Squirrel, I will have to balance on your shoulders. Come, in it,' Innit beckons.

I then help Innit up onto Squirrel, he is like an acrobat. And then there is light. Innit jumps down and we go back into the hallway.

Squirrel carries on speaking excitedly as we stand at the bottom of the stairs; 'the main bedroom is mine because I cracked the squat.

There is one room left which you will have to share, or you can take it in turns to sleep in the front room. Go upstairs.'

'Sara can have that room, in it,' Innit announces, 'I will go and put in the light bulb for her.'

I smile at Squirrel widely as Innit goes up with another bulb in hand. I now have my own room and a sort of home.

'Thanks, Squirrel, for facilitating this opportunity for us,' Squirrel looks slightly confused for a few seconds, 'I really didn't fancy another night in the park.' I feel cheerful. 'Squirrel, one four pack of lager is for you and the other is to share between me and Innit,' I tell him. Instead of champagne we've super strength lager to celebrate with. On the can it reads 'serve the lager chilled'; I can't imagine this making any difference.

'Innit stole us the light bulbs, and you accompanied us,' Squirrel informs me, 'this is a joint effort.' Squirrel adds, 'we are borrowing the house; we want to leave it hopefully in a better state if that's possible, that's the rules to squatting.'

'Yeah right Squirrel, in it,' Innit answers sarcastically.

Collectively we go to investigate the kitchen, this has a table and chairs in and beige doors on the kitchen cabinets. Innit takes us through, pointing out all the amenities in an amusing way.

'This is where we'll put our dishwasher, in it...Squirrel that's you, in it.'

Squirrel explains that someone needs to be in the house constantly to stop the real owners entering and changing the locks. Squirrel is happy in the house now he has his alcohol.

Squirrel places a hand on my shoulder and says, 'I know you don't know us that well, but we like you Sara and we can sense that you're having a hard time and we just want to help.'

Innit needs to go out to get drugs, so I go with him, promising to be quick. Innit grabs one four pack of lagers with his bad hand, wincing, and goes and hides them somewhere, Squirrel has no morals where alcohol is concerned, he returns after a couple of minutes.

'You should've looked at your room first, in it,' he advises and then opens the front door and ushers me out. 'We are going to have to walk to Easton,' Innit explains, 'no one else will be on at this time.'

We wander back down to the shops and up towards Gloucester road, turning the opposite way at the traffic lights and heading down to more newsagents with bright lit up signs and turn just before them, to the right, and going downhill till we reach City road. We cross the road and Mickey, Innit's friend, is asleep outside another cafe across from us. Mickey is swaddled in his sleeping bag. And go around some winding short roads, noticing the top of the steeple of the old church, which is lit up purple, blue, and red, protruding up to the night sky over the top of the other buildings. This looks awe inspiring. We turn into Portland Place with its Georgian buildings and central green with trees surrounded by black railings.

Rene is there, standing waiting for a punter, we go and talk to her.

'Rene, we just found a squat, in it, we gotta stay off the streets cos of Kev,' Innit smiles, looking chuffed.

'Respect,' Rene says, 'I'll be around.'

I follow Innit past a green in front of a huge building and through terrace houses until we get to a bridge cutting across the M32. Innit's charming towards me; this is contrary to the pugnacious attitude he can show others, resulting in violence; only with justification.

'This is Easton, in it,' Innit notifies me.

We parade through the streets at speed, go past the leisure centre and The Wild Goose, a free food place according to Innit, we go up the main road past the high-rises, pubs, and more terrace houses. Turning left up the slope and right. There's a magnificent mosque here with beautiful green lighting covering the building behind the external, gold, patterned glass, and a dome roof like an Indian palace. We've walked quite a distance.

'Now I need to meet someone, in it.'

Innit strolls off down the road. He's going to reconvene with me in ten minutes. He doesn't enlighten me about who he's meeting, which is probably for the best, and I don't ask. I'm starting to know my way around Bristol and am becoming inured to city life. Innit and Squirrel have helped me by educating me on areas and road names. Innit approaches me at speed.

'Alright darling, do you come here often? Come on hurry up, in it,' he grins, looking at me with his big oval brown eyes, his blonde hair all ruffled.

Innit is flying along. We start moving briskly. Walking off the slight chill in the air. We go through the streets full of terraced houses and cross the busy main road again. We go up the road leading up to Brunswick Square (so Innit points out) and up past a nightclub. Now on the lit-up Gloucester Road, Innit wanders by the twenty-four-hour shop and the sign falls to the floor, knocked by someone, and makes a resounding crash. Innit jumps and I burst into laughter. Jokingly, I slap him playfully around the head.

'Oi, in it,' he retorts and tries to slap me back as I run away.

I like busy streets at night, they are alluring and are different in comparison to my childhood experiences. I've the fearlessness of youth. We arrive at the traffic lights at a crossing, firstly passing two big cafes, one with Mickey asleep in the doorway, the other is next to the drinkers steps, leading up to the entrance to an derelict building, with boarded up arched windows, Squirrel sits there sometimes; in this area of Bristol, buildings can stay unoccupied and neglected. The sky is lightning, the sun is coming up, I see a mishmash of bright coloured graffiti, on top of more bright graffiti, which has created artworks within themselves like an enigma.

I cross the road and immediately turn left into the street leading downhill to local shops. As you turn into the street, boards are on the right around the corrugated buildings and someone has written on one of the boards 'love your life' in green, outlined in black with bright orange squiggles in-between the letters over a lighter green background. I like this, it reaffirms my optimistic propensity, for now anyway, with my metaphorical pink-tinted sunglasses on. We walk past the graffiti of a five-armed-alien and surreal cat. Once in front of the newsagents, we cross the paved area and head uphill again. The steepness slows us down. Finally, we get to our orange door. I knock and Squirrel opens this in a grouchy manner and shuffles back inside.

We follow Squirrel and I go to place my bag in my bedroom. I flick the light switch and my new room is illuminated by the bare bulb which Innit sorted out, bless him. My room must have been a girl's nursery because the wallpaper is pink and covered in fairies and flowers. There's a thick cream carpet which adds warmth to the place and shelves which we move into the hallway. Innit beckons me out and gives me a tour of the upstairs.

Squirrel's room has a double bed frame up against the wall and bare floorboards, maybe, I have the better deal. There's a white flatpack chest-of-drawers in the corner; one of the drawer fronts is hanging off. We discover Squirrel standing looking out of his window. Squirrel's room has mahogany walls. This place is luxurious in comparison to where we slept last night; it has a roof, walls, windows and doors.

'Thanks Squirrel,' I say, he had managed to get into the house.

The front room has a bay window and open fire, the kitchen is long and has been enlarged with an extension leading through to the garden; luckily this has no deadlock and the key has rusted into the lock so we can open the door. I go to view the overgrown garden; this has obviously been lovingly cared for once. I can see there is an orange rose bush near the tall fence on one side of the garden. I pick some to put in my room, trying to avoid the thorns.

The house smells musty and needs airing. I find a squash bottle in the kitchen and get Squirrel to cut the top of it, making a vase. Squirrel has got a present for me, a sleeping mat. He has one for all of us. He got them for free from a Christian charity. It is amazing how resourceful you become when you have no possession. He also goes around the house with a bunch of lit joss sticks, waving them into the corners of each room. My mum used to put out potpourri in the bathroom, not quite the same thing.

'Thanks again Squirrel, you have thought of everything,' I say. 'I really appreciate all this.'

I'm glad that I acquired him the lager. Innit and Squirrel are pottering about fixing things. I am sitting on the kitchen counter swinging my legs and looking out of the windows when Innit approaches me.

'Thanks too, Innit, for being a friend to me since I've been here,' I say, feeling a bit shy for some reason.

I grab him by the arm, being careful of his injured hand, and jump down from the counter to re-join Squirrel. We all sit around in a circle, on our sleeping bags, and talk in the (light yellow coloured) open-planned, oblong kitchen and dining room.

Innit gets out an asthma inhaler, he places foil over the top of it and makes some holes in the foil with a board pin he finds on the floor. He takes his time due to not being able to fully bend his hand. He starts to save up some ash from a cigarette to place over the foil; the crack he will then place on top of the ash. Squirrel uses his glass pipe with wire wool, no ash is needed.

We smoke a pipe of crack each and the room fills with smoke, so we open the door for a few seconds. I am becoming used to the taste and aren't coughing anymore which is quite worrying. The trouble with crack is after one pipe you subsequently want another immediately. Innit gets the larger out and passes a can around to each of us, allowing us to calm down a bit. I have on my metaphorical pink-tinted sunglasses on and instantly feel better, everything is awash with pink. The drug has opened us up and we start to tell each other our stories; after all, we are now living together.

Innit starts telling me his life story, 'I was brought up by my mum, in it. I never met my dad, in it, we moved around a lot. On the estate, drugs were everywhere. I started riding around on my bike delivering crack to people for this Crew, in it. When they gave me heroin to deliver, I kept stealing bits, in it. I was tempted to do some because someone told me it was the best buzz and I was upset because my mum had moved without telling me, in it. I had my first taste of heroin at twelve, in it. I didn't get that good a buzz so I kept trying a bit every day to see if it would get better. I got hooked, in it.'

'The Crew I worked for put me up, in it, because I was stealing their drugs, they kicked me out, in it. I got expelled from school, in it; I went in feeling like shite after sleeping in the bus station and another boy wound me up, so I smashed a chair over his head, in it. I was sleeping rough at the age of fourteen.' I moved closer to Innit feeling sad for him; I led down, putting my head on his thigh.

'What about you then Squirrel,' I ask. 'Tell us some more of your story.'

'You know it all already, I told you the first day we met, I was brought up in Care and ran away.' He smiles, looking at me through his messy dreadlocks. 'I am just biding time until the world as we know it changes, and learning as many survival skills as possible. Society is going to collapse and we are all going to have to go back to the old ways, most people are dead men walking and they don't even know it.' 'What do you mean Squirrel,' I ask astonished.

'Don't go scaring Sarah with your thoughts, in it. '

'I have dreamt about these things Sara, don't want to bore you, tell us your story Sara, we know you had a partner that you don't like talking about, so Innit reckons. Tell us some of *your* story,' I notice Innit is also studying me intently.

'I have had quite a normal life. I grew up in a nice house near Camberley. What else can I tell you; I don't want to feel like I'm rubbing salt into the wounds,' I reply, still a bit astonished at Squirrels ramblings.

'It can't be that normal or you wouldn't be here, in it,' Innit answers, 'a dead partner, in it?'

'Yes, I suppose. Look now things are still quite raw, when I want to tell you I will, I promise.' A picture of my partner's face comes into my mind and my eyes begin to water.

'When you feel ready to talk, we are here, in it, it's better to talk about things, in it,' Innit advises me. 'I'm a good listener, in it.'

'Don't bottle things up, Sara,' Squirrel advises.

'Okay, I will tell you,' I say, 'my partner died a short while ago, he died from mysterious circumstances.'

'What happened, in it,' Innit asks sombrely.

'They couldn't find a reason,' I reply, 'they think it was a brain haemorrhage because he was a boxer, he was twenty-two and I had to see him on Life Support and was told he was brain dead. We had to turn this off.' I start crying heavily, Innit and Squirrel come over and give me a hug.

When I have stopped crying, we all decide to go to sleep.

'It's going to be weird sleeping in a house,' Squirrel explains, 'i'm going to have to open all the windows in my room or I will get claustrophobic. I can't hack heating, so it's lucky we ain't got any.'

Squirrel runs up the stairs. I hear his clumpy boots on each step.

Innit puts an arm around me and this feels nice. 'Come and stay in the front room, in it.' 'I'm okay, I have to get used to my new room. Remember to wash and rebandage your hand,' I say and give Innit a peck on the lips. Innit looks disappointed at the bottom of the stairs.

'I'm going to have another hit, in it,' Innit states.

'Can I have one Innit,' I ask, I am emotionally worn out due to my conversation about my partner. 'I feel upset and like I want to die.'

'Sara, heroin is shit, if you get a habit your fucked, in it,' Innit replies, with a serious look.

'I won't get one, I promise,' I answer, tears welling up in my eyes again.

Innit stares at me intently and purses his lips together and shakes his head, 'you can't tell Squirrel, he wouldn't be pleased, in it.'

'I won't,' I reply, looking at Innit in earnest.

'Come then,' Innit says and waves me into the front room with his hand.

I follow, Innit's room is bare, we sit on his sleeping mat and he gets his kit bag full of clean syringes, spoons, filters and citric acid, and starts to cook up a bag of H.

'Sarah, I'm only giving you ten mil, I don't want you overdosing on me,' Innit replies and draws the stuff into the syringe.

He sits down next to me and pulls one of his shoelaces around my arm, this hurts slightly.

He jabs the needle in, and this is painful, he can't get a vein straight away.

'I forgot how shit women's veins are, in it,' he retorts and shows me his bulging veins.

He then finds one and draws up, blood flows into the syringe, he holds this steady and pushes slowly until this is empty. I lay back whilst he gets himself. I feel the nice feeling flow around my body, taking over my mind, I am sinking into oblivion, my mind is clear, at peace, I feel superb. I'm wearing my pink-tinted sunglasses. I could be flying in the beautiful blue sky, time no longer has any meaning, my vision is blurred. I have never felt so good. I look around for Innit and see him relaxing back beside me. Nothing matters, nothing hurts. We both close our eyes and enjoy. I must have fallen asleep. When I wake, I have no idea how long I have slept for. I have been led on my arm which is now dead. Innit is next to me, I check that he is breathing. He is.

I drift comfortably upstairs to my room. I lay down on the camping mat and get into my sleeping bag, feeling like a caterpillar that's metamorphosed into a butterfly. I go to sleep when most people are waking up surrounded by pink fairy covered wallpaper. I take off my sweatshirt and put it under my head as a cushion and fall asleep almost immediately.

Chapter Seven; The Pyramid

I woke up late, totally disorientated.

I notice that Innit isn't in his room. I peek through the doorway. I arise and amble downstairs to see where he and Squirrel are. Firstly, getting a drink of water. I need hydration. I go through to the kitchen and notice that there is no door or any kitchen cabinet doors. Then I peek into the lounge and notice that the door is missing as well, this is a mystery. I enter the room fearfully. I can hear Squirrel snoring. I go in to explore further and observe little tiny flakes of sawdust on the floor. What has ensued? This is a conundrum. Is this a dream?

I immerse myself into the room and realise that now every piece of furniture, doors, and all our electrical equipment (Squirrel had found a T.V. and radio on the street and brought them in), have disappeared, like magic, and what takes up the entirety of the room, in its place, is a pyramid, three dimensional and enchanting. Examining the building material of the pyramid, I can see that this is made up of tiny bits consisting of all these things and pieces of lager cans, the lager cans have been crushed and torn in half, and are now part of the pyramid's composition and gleam gold in the sun, there are wires, bits of door, plastic and even small speakers and circuit boards all piled up to make this clearly defined shape. The shape is perfect. The Egyptian couldn't do better. Replicating one of the Seven Wonders of the World. The funniest thing is that the pyramid is in the front room and Innit is asleep on top of it, moulded into the tiny fragments, Squirrel's asleep on the floor besieged by beer cans. What has happened? I pinch myself and it hurts, this must be real?

How had Innit and Squirrel managed to build such a perfect representation?

I'm astounded by Innit and Squirrel's version. I've never seen such a surprising art piece. The catch is now we have no furniture and there would be a lot of cleaning up to do. We could charge people an entrance fee to see the piece like a sideshow. I wish that we could preserve this for eternity, like Jesus, here till the end of time.

This pyramid is genius. I see Innit stirring and he rises to a sitting position. He smiles at me.

'What have you been up to,' I ask, still wondering if I'm dreaming. 'What's all this about?'

Innit answers, 'Squirrel couldn't sleep, he woke me up, I ain't really slept, in it, we left you asleep, in it. Squirrel and I got hammered, he had a couple of bottles of white cider hidden in his room, in it,' Innit smiles. 'We wanted to make you something, in it.'

'You certainly have done that, the pyramid is fantastically amazing,' I say, 'you two are illuminating. How did I sleep through all of this?' I ask Innit, confused.

'You were tired, and I closed the bedroom door, in it. Squirrel and I were arguing as to whether aliens built the pyramids because they're so accurate in their dimension, in it. I bet Squirrel that I could prove humans could build one, but we had no material like sand, in it.
Then, Squirrel had the bright idea,' (I imagine a light bulb flashing above Squirrel's head),
'after a lot of cider, that we'd smash everything up into sand like pieces, in it. Which I instantly agreed to,' Innit smiles. 'It's a good one, in it,' Innit stands up on the pyramid and touches the ceiling, he wobbles slightly and sits back down. 'I wanted to see the pyramids before I die, in it.'

'Please don't say that,' I reply, dismayed, 'help me up,' I reach out my hand for him to assist me, and carefully sit by Innit on top of the pyramid, trying not to disturb any of the components as I'm pulled gently up. 'Innit am I dreaming.'

'Of course not, in it,' Innit responds and slaps me.

'Oi,' I exclaim, rubbing my face, I wasn't dreaming, that stung.

'Just getting you back for the other day outside the shop, in it,' Innit declares and grins.

'Innit can you please stop being so final,' I ask in earnest, 'I don't want anyone else dying on me.'

'I'm a drug addict, Sara, in it, we don't survive very long, in it.'

Innit's smiling, but I notice that he looks pale and his skin is clammy.

'I thought you two were going to leave the house in a good condition,' I say, trying to change the subject.

Innit is now laughing hysterically. I notice that he looks pale and his skin is clammy, he almost wretches.

'I have got to go and score before I throw up Sara. I used my morning stuff really early with you, I always do that, fucking idiot that I am, in it. I hate it when this happens. I probably won't even make it to get it, I will have to crawl on all fours down the road, in it. Why the fuck do I do it to myself, I am ill as fuck, what a dickhead, in it.'

'Come on, I will help in this pursuit, put your arm around my shoulder and you can lean on me,' I reply and Innit does exactly that (Love that song, good words).

Innit looks dirty, there are blood spots on his jeans, his nails are dirty, his hair is greasy, his eyes and face are still lovely, but I wish he was cleaner.

'Innit, why don't you go and have a bath and relax instead,' I ask.

'No way Sara, I'm getting stuff, I have to have my drugs,' Innit announces, grabbing his shoes and I also put mine on. Innit's problematic drug misuse is very real, he's unyielding in his quest, his belligerence immerses me back into reality.

Chapter Eight; The Dragon

We come out into the fresh air and march down the hill.

'We are going round to Trevor's in the high-rises, in it.'

   We wander back down to the shops and up towards Gloucester Road, turning by the charity shop on the corner. There's a huge, red, Welsh Dragon, made from metal, on top of the cafe opposite us. Someone has hurled blue paint over it and the dragon's face has blue streaks. How did they manage to get up there; maybe they climbed out of one of the surrounding house windows? This seems like a lot of effort just to deface a red Welsh Dragon, unless they thought this to be a metaphor for The Devil. I wonder if The Devil is a shapeshifter who can morph into anyone on Earth, how creepy would that be?

"And the great dragon was cast out, that old serpent, called the Devil, and Satan, which deceiveth the whole world: he was cast out into the earth, and his angels were cast out with him" (Rev.12:9). This excerpt from The Bible goes through my head for some reason.

   The traffic is hectic here. The washed-out chequerboard pavement's polka dotted with old chewing gum, like a contemporary artwork. We head up the hill, past the cafe with the dragon and past a bin with the words 'do not be bitter' written in white on it; I like this, it's metaphorically showing you to throw away all your bitterness in life. I wish that were possible. We pass the skips with scribbled writing all over them and a triangle symbol with an eye in the centre painted on the wall. Weave through the parked cars and past a runner in his neon green jacket, and then notice an amazing graffiti piece to the left of us.

A house has a huge tree covering it and on each branch are different things; there's an alien, a wizard, a scarab beetle, the anarchist sign, Clifton Suspension Bridge, an Egyptian god (Anubis, the jackal-headed man), the yin yang sign (ancient Chinese philosophy), and a flower. This graffiti piece encompasses a lot, humanity is diverse and interesting. All of us are desperately searching for clarity to enforce some meaning in our lives.

We cross the road and head towards another council block, and past the phone box with all the windows kicked out and covered in paint.

'What's the point in that?' I ask Innit, looking miffed.

'The police tap that phone box because they see it being used by us lot, in it, someone made it unusable, in it,' he responds.

'Why don't you buy a pay-as-you-go mobile?' I answer.

'I always lose them, or they get stolen, in it.'

There's a sprayed bomb on the side of the high-rise with an anarchist sign by it. On the right, in the distance, a crane is poking up from the tops of the buildings from the development by Castle park. We pass the garages, and the hostel with a man sitting smoking on the steps, and pass the rectangular green, penned in by black railings, with beautiful tall trees, and up to our destination, the high-rise, colour scheme of red and grey. We pass an abandoned shopping trolley and coffee table and venture up to the wooden door with security glass as an old couple comes out. Innit stops and presses the buzzer on the silver intercom.

'In it,' he answers.

'Come up,' the crackling voice expresses and then I hear the door buzz and Innit forcefully pushes it open.

We go into the roomy hallway of the concrete block, with the questionable colour scheme, and up in the silver lift to the top floor. There is a marvellous view. We get to a door. The painted door has multiple messages scratched onto it, one of the scratched messages reads 'NO FUTURE'. Innit knocks, we hear multiple locks being undone, and the door opens. We are let in by a man.

'T.J,' Innit says.

'Who the fuck are you with Bruv? You shouldn't be bringing people with you.' T.J. states, he has longish blonde hair and a bulky build, he's wearing a plain T-shirt and jeans.

'Come on Bruv, this is my Mrs, in it.'

'Oh, okay, but ask me next time.'

'I will, in it,' we all make our way into the front room of the shadowy flat and sit down on the sofa, 'where's Trevor, in it?

T.J smiles and answers, 'I've relegated him to his room, can't put up with it Bruv, he's just constantly talking to himself.'

'So, you've taken over his flat then,' Innit responds, 'you know Trevor's schizophrenic, in it. He's been arguing with the queen, in his head, since he was twelve years old, in it.'

'Yeah, he calls her Regina,' T.J. reveals and smirks. T.J gets up and goes to the front room door. 'Trevor, come out here and say hello to Innit.'

Whilst we are waiting for Trevor to make an appearance, I glance around the room. I notice that the person, T.J., is sitting on an armchair in front of two T.V. screens; one has a picture of the external front door to the high-rise flats, obviously they have wired up a camera, and the other screen is playing pornography. I sit in stunned silence; this place is horrible and squalid.

Innit notices me looking at the screens, 'turn the Porn off Bruv,' he requests.

'What's the matter, don't you like sex?' T.J. elicits, laughing.

Then Trevor enters with a smile on his face and a weird look in his eyes, and the pornography is forgotten about. He is older, big and round.

'Trevor, in it,' Innit says and grins, looking up at the man, 'you okay, the queen leaving you alone these days?'

Trevor proceeds to sit beside Innit on the sofa, his hair is sticking up, looking punkish,' no, Regina is a fucking slag,' he proclaims, 'she's a Borge alien, mark two, she walks through walls. I can speak Borge,' with that Trevor faces us and sticks his tongue out and moves it from side to side, 'that means hello in Borge,' he discloses.

'Erm...' Innit is stuck for words, he turns from Trevor to T.J., who is watching the televisions intently, and asks, 'erm T.J., can I get one of each?'

'Only got whites Bruv,' he clarifies.

'For fucks sake, yeah give me one of those, we have to be quick Bruv, in it.'

T.J. passes Innit the small ball of cling film and rises out of his seat to see us out of the flat, we follow him to the front door and Innit turns to him and says, 'thanks, Bruv.'

I turn to say goodbye to Trevor, and he peers at me and says, 'I have been treated like a child since I was five years old and I am still not happy about it.'

'Okay.' I say to placate him, uneasy about his state of mind, and we make our way out of the flat. T.J. shows us out of the multi-bolted door which reminds me of prison; or what I would expect this to be like. I notice the irony; they would be kept at Her Majesty's Pleasure soon.

'Laters, in it.'

We hear the locks being done back up on the way out.

I feel a bit sorry for Trevor, he won't have that place for long, in it, his flat has been turned into a drug shop, T.J. runs things hot as fuck, you can get stuff at any time of day,' Innit explains, pauses, and looks at me intently, 'sorry for calling you my Mrs, but he'll leave you alone if he thinks that, in it.'

'I understand Innit, thanks,' I reply, 'I feel sad for Trevor, he isn't well.'

'No,' Innit retorts, 'I want to take the Queen round one day to answer for herself, in it.'

We rapidly walk back in the squats direction and go along Ashley Road past the newsagents. Innit is now walking doubled up. He starts to wretch again. The newsagents are open.

Innit sees two of his friends loitering outside one of the shops, one calls out to him, 'Innit you look like shit.'

'Thanks, in it,' Innit answers sarcastically, 'you like stating the obvious Mickey.'

Mickey grins, he has a baseball cap on and is making exaggerated hand movements as if he is a rapper on stage, 'cool, what happened to you last week in court for nicking that sandwich?'

'It was funny as fuck, I turned up at court and got my needles confiscated straight away because of the metal detectors and, when they called me into court, I was so hungry that the usher turned into roast chicken, I walked into court pissing myself laughing, I couldn't stop, they were going to bail me but I had a letter of support from the drugs services. I told them I had problems that I needed addressing, in it, and their response was to fine me eighty pounds, in it, like they will ever get that, in it,' Innit smirks.

'At least that's better than last time, you were so out of it on Valium that you were gouging out in the dock, they could've given you Life and you wouldn't have given a fuck,' Mickey laughs, 'do you want me to ring someone? We are scoring anyway?' Mickey asks.

'Yeah that would be great, in it, I need one B.'

Mickey dials a number on his mobile and starts a conversation with the person on the other end.

-Yeah two whites and four brown, that's right,' he turns to Innit and asks, 'Innit you want one B right?'

'Yep, in it.'

-Can we have six for thirty-five or forty?

-Okay, forty it is, safe Bruv, see you in five minutes.

The call clicks to an end.

We walk along and stand by a square green space in the urbanised Bristol, waiting for the person to turn up with stuff. Then a young woman accompanied by a huge guy comes to wait with us, another man is with them in a wheelchair, making a roll up, he only has half a leg.

Innit motions to the tobacco and asks, 'can I have a roll up, in it?'

The man in the wheelchair passes this up to Innit. As Innit stands making one, the massive guy walks over and says to the man in the wheelchair, 'if you pass my baccy out I will box you in the face.'

Then he walks up to the skinny young woman and orders, 'stay here or I will box you in the face.'

He looks at me with interest. I stay quiet. He talks to Innit with respect and states, 'if this guy doesn't turn up, I will box him in the face.'

This seems to be the only sentence he can muster, and his minions do as he commands obediently. They all seem scared of him which isn't surprising.

Mickey phones the dealer and lets us know that we need to go to another location because the police are about. The big guy orders his friends to come 'or he will box them in the face'. We march down and pass the Bakery.

Innit instructs, 'go and stand up the alleyway and wait for me, in it, the dealer will freak out if there are too many people and he doesn't know you yet, in it.'

He walks me some of the way.

'They seem like intelligent successful people,' I say when we are out of ear shot, nodding in the direction of the people we had just left.

'In it.'

Innit leaves me and runs back in their direction. I'm not enjoying myself. I wish I could get Innit off the drugs and around some decent people, not being snobby, just not liking the desperate characters I am meeting. Well, hopefully I can go back to my normal life and have a home soon.

I feel disoriented due to my disturb sleep. We drift past the bright lights of a fish and chip shop. I wait for Innit. He returns with Mickey and we go back to the squat, passing one house with the words 'Welcome to Montpelier' across the top, with black outlines of birds and flowers covering the colourful front, before that is a health food shop with a metal structure consisting of hearts on the end of metal pipes stuck along a zigzagging metal bar, like a giant wavy caterpillar, hanging off the top of the building. This is a fascinating place. Standing by the door of the newsagents, I notice a man with a friendly face behind the counter, a restaurant opposite, and a sparkling gold sign catches my eye further down and reflects the words 'Thai Café' on its lilac walls and is lit up like a Christmas tree.

'Innit I forgot to tell you,' Mickey informs Innit as we walk up the hill, 'you know Feet, he was in Bath and went to get some copper wire to weigh in and bloody sawed through a live wire, he got fifty thousand volts going through his body and almost died, he only survived because he had thick rubber-soled boots on and the current couldn't earth, it shot out of his head and burnt his long hair on the way out.'

Innit started to laugh again, 'I haven't seen Feet for ages, is he okay, in it?'

Mickey responds smiling, 'of course he isn't okay, he has melted half his arm, it's in a transparent carrier bag up to his elbow, it's going to take ages to recover, lucky he is so big, this would have killed someone else.'

Innit is hysterically laughing now, 'Fucking idiot, I am going to have to go see him, he is living in Bath now in it?'

'Yeah, he was only around for the day and to pick up some stuff, next time I see him I will tell him you were asking after him, fucking idiot.'

Jay and Innit laugh for a few minutes, tears in both of their eyes.

'Life's funny as fuck sometimes, in it.'

We go through the garden and in the front door and straight up into my small room. Squirrel is asleep still beside the pyramid. Mickey, like Innit, has a kit bag as well, the only things inside are syringes, pipes, and other drug paraphernalia. We all have a pipe on Innit's asthma inhaler, feeling great, we chat with ease.

'What are you doing today Mickey, in it?'

'Going to make some money Bruv.' Mickey answers.

'I will come with you, in it,' Innit responds, 'Sara are you okay with that?'

'Yes, that's fine,' I reply.

'Sara, go and find Rene for me,' Mickey says, 'I worry about her,' he reveals and pulls his baseball cap off, runs his hands through his hair and then puts it back on, the peak slightly facing the side.

'I will come out with you guys and see what she's doing,' I reply, I want to speak to Rene anyway, I want some female company and a laugh. It would be boring in the squat by myself waiting for Squirrel to awaken

'We can go down to the Bear Pit and see if Rene is there and if she aint, you could go and look for her in Portland Square, in it,' Innit suggests, kneeling on the floor, pulling his kit back towards him and getting out his tools of his trade.

'I don't wanna take you Sara cos we are gonna be doing dodgy stuff, in it,' Innit looks at me with resignation and smiles. 'Hopefully I will come back with funds.'

Innit starts to cook up a hit for us all to share. He puts the heroin into the spoon with the citric acid, draws up the water and rips off a small piece of filter. Mickey hands Innit a clean syringe and Innit draws him and Mickey equal amounts, I get less in my syringe. Innit injects himself first and his eyes keep shutting and his head keeps sinking to the floor. Mickey gets his hit by going straight into the top of his arm, or the 'blood bank' as he calls it.

I feel annoyed, I want to be like them. I want my pink-tinted sunglasses on and the world to brighten.

'Innit get me please,' I say and put on my tourniquet, and sit and wait patiently as Innit tries to get a vein on me, he keeps forgetting what he's doing and drops the syringe. Mickey is watching amused.

'I'll do it,' he says, he is more coherent.

'Sara, you need to learn to do this yourself,' Mickey says, 'I will show you some places if you want, I'm going to get your 'blood bank',' he says and goes vertically into the top of my arm where my muscle is and gets me first time, he has the knowledge of anatomy of a doctor.

'Thanks Mickey,' I reply, feeling the warm rush as the drug goes through my veins and to my brain. I lounge back on my sleeping bag, blissfully sinking into the floor. Pink-tinted sunglasses firmly on. After a while of lying back and enjoying the buzz, I can hear Mickey and Innit chatting in the background but this seems distant and my head keeps sinking to the floor, then I feel slightly alert and then sinking again into a warm pink duvet and pillows.

Chapter Nine; The Introduction

'Sara, we're going to go now, in it,' Innit announces and pulls me up off the bed and I drift along beside them.

We go up the sloping street with a relaxed café with plants in the window. We pass the newsagent on the corner which curves around. The corner shop has graffiti all over the blinds; tags are everywhere, on the walls, road signs and even the shop's white van..van...van. My eyes shut and I start to sway.

'Sara...hello, in it,' Innit brings me around.

As we turn, a corrugated iron building meets my eyes with a surreal blue cat and a pink alien with six arms and three blue eyes. We go past the bar and further up to the steps where the Street Drinkers sit. And, by The Art House café, with its leather sofas and walls full of art, we stop at a set of traffic lights and Innit ushers me across the busy dual carriage road, pulling my arm to get me across safely. We cross over and turn right, seeing the rabbit hutches.

Innit hooks his arms into mine carefully so he doesn't hurt his hand. He walks with his hand constantly up, this is still bandaged, but now this is off white in colour and streaked with dirt and blood. We pass the lamppost with shredded up fliers on, and go past the bar forecourt, with benches and chairs, and a giant mushroom with a weird, spiky alien creature smoking a bong on top. I pass the beige sofa which is on the street beneath a quote by Martin Luther King, 'Injustice anywhere is a threat to justice'. Good words. We go down the slope to the Bear Pit.

Mickey stands chatting to some people. He looks sweaty and white. One of the people is rapping, 'why should I do what authorities tell me to, cos they do wrong too', and someone else is doing beatbox. I study the Bear Pit. It has greenery, yet is encased by buildings and roads, you can see the traffic lights and signs overhead...overhead....My eyes shut again and I have to slap my face to wake myself up. There are three people asleep on the floor by the free table-tennis table. We are surrounded by windows.

We approach the group standing by the green bank with the beautiful willow tree.

'Has anyone seen Rene,' Mickey enquiries, the group are sitting with guitars and cans in hand.

'Portland square Bruv,' one answers.

'Sara go see she's alright,' Mickey asks. 'Safe Sara.'

See you both later,' I reply and scale the slope back up to Gloucester road.

I'm feeling more awake now. And further up past the chemist and down towards

Brunswick Square, I see Rene sitting by herself on the bench. I go over to her, and she sees me and instinctively smiles. She looks happy. She's picking stuff out of her teeth with her fingernails.

'I just had a client, gonna go score,' Rene explains, 'come on.'

As we walk, I start to broach the subject of how she made her money, 'how did you start your current employment?' I ask, peering at her.

Rene laughs. 'Well, they were recruiting at the job centre and I thought I would apply. I liked the hours.'

'Seriously, what happened?' I ask in earnest. 'You are too good to be doing this and I'm not judging you at all when I say this.'

'I'm okay,' she responds. 'I need the money and that's all there is to it. I'll stop one day.' We didn't know each other very well and she is guarded about herself which is understandable.

Rene takes me around to meet one of her *friend's*. He lives in one of the blocks of flats off Gloucester road, we go up the hill and past more graffiti and into the lift. We have a laugh and I realise that she resembles one of my friends from my old school. I don't think of her as a sex-worker, she is just like a normal female of our age but she has just been through more and is controlled by drugs; like my friends at home are controlled by men and food but a million times worse. The important thing is that Rene is a nice person, or she seems so to me. Rene presses the floor button. There are numerous floors; I can't believe that the council can put people so high up. The lift starts and we stand facing the silver doors waiting for them to open. Rene fills me in on what we are doing.

'I'm getting a couple of stones,' she explains.

I have learnt that the name 'stone' is another name for crack cocaine. Rene is well addicted to crack cocaine, it is early and she's already thinking of her first fix. We move along the open corridor to a flat. I peer over the barrier to ascertain how high up we are. There is a small playground out the front of the building, but this is deserted, a dodgy couple are selling things out of their carrier bags. Raising my head, I survey the view of houses and roads, occasionally broken up by a small stretch of green. We come to a battered door and Rene knocks. The curtains twitch at the window and I see the blurred shape of someone looking out.

'We are just going to pop in quickly.' Rene advises and taps on the door. After a few seconds, the door opens, and a big guy stands looking at us. He has a red string vest which exposes his abdominal muscles. He is fit.

'Who's dis?' He asks warily.

Rene introduces me. I feel uncomfortable.

'My half-sister, Sara, she's staying with me at the moment. Our Mums kicked her out.'

'Yu hav a sister,' he exclaims in surprise. 'Come.' He leads us into his front room. This is at the end of the corridor, past the kitchen and bedroom. He has a massive flat screen T.V. and black leather sofas. There is a big pine coffee table in the centre of the room. One wall is decorated with black and silver wallpaper, the other walls are red. The framed Jamaican flag is up on one of them, the proud lion looks down at me, demanding respect. T-Bone Is listening to reggae through two big speakers, these have massive bass bins that look like they have been used in street carnivals.

'Wot yu want?' He enquires.

'Hav yu got a lickle ting for us?' Rene replies.

T-Bone kisses his teeth. 'Yu ring me next time or yu'll get nu-ting, do hear,' and then reluctantly hands over the small ball of cling film. He looks over at me. 'I'm T-Bone, if yu need any boom ting yu come and see me,' he advises and smiles a big pearly white smile and then looks back at Rene and asks, 'where are yu gonna smoke it?'

'We'll find somewhere,' Rene replies.

He gets out a pipe and offers this to her. The pipe is like Squirrel's, made of transparent glass. 'Yu aint gonna smoke de ting on ma stairs. Me not want yu hoting up ma yard. Just smoke de ting here.'

So, we did. I feel like I am flying. This wakes me up and gives me energy, I can handle life, a plaster is stuck over my depression. My pink-tinted sunglasses are placed firmly on.

'Your sister reminds me of someone,' T-Bone states, 'me can't quite tink who it tis...ah yes, a girl from de Sweet House. There is some-ting similar about de face.'

'W-what's The Sweet House?' I ask, curious.

'One of ma business contacts runs de place, it's a strip club. Why, yu tinking of doing some-ting like dat. I hav de address if yu want.'

'Yes, thanks,' I respond and T-Bone hands me a business card.

'Tis not far from here, if yu wanna job just say I sent yu.' T-Bone advises. 'They will pay yu in cash.'

'Thanks T-Bone, appreciated,' I answer, 'yes I do need a job.'

T-Bone gives me directions to the club and Rene and T-Bone go to speak in the kitchen. Then Rene quickly goes out of the room. I get up off the sofa and follow her into the corridor to tell her I'm departing, thinking I can make a quick getaway, I knock on the bathroom door.

'Come in,' Rene says.

I enter the bathroom. She puts her finger up to her mouth. She is standing with her skirt up and her pants are around her ankles. I see that she has a big oblong package covered in cling film and is unbecomingly shoving this up inside her.

'Gotta drop something off for T-Bone,' she explains, 'keep that to yourself Sara, I mean it,'

Rene scowls, 'if I find out you have said anything to anyone you'll be in trouble.'

'I won't Rene,' I promise.

She has finished, the package has disappeared, and she is pulling up her pants and down her skirt, 'hurry up,' she says.

I wash in T-Bone's bathroom and do my makeup. I get my makeup bag out and do my eyeliner and put on some black eyeshadow and some lip-gloss, pulling my plaited hair back into a ponytail. I need a job. I know a Jamaican man in Bath who gets paid to teach children poetry. He goes all around the world. I think this is much better than selling drugs. This is only legal when the CIA does it.

I leave Rene there smoking and leave T-Bone's place. I feel pleased to be walking in the open air. I'm sauntering down the road above Gloucester road. I walk briskly in the direction that T-Bone showed me, passing the hospital with the metal sculpture. I turn left, opposite this, and go down some steps and along an alleyway with walls covered in graffiti, and curve round, eventually coming out in the centre by the statue of the cloaked man on the beautifully carved horse. I pass offices, and on the central island, surrounded by busy main roads, is the war memorial, the water feature and the statue of Neptune holding his long spear and surveying the harbour.

As I'm walking, cars dash past causing exhaust fumes to fill the air. Bristol's certainly a busy city. I go past an old Greek inspired building with columns; this is what I like about Bristol, there are modern high-rises (the outside made completely from glass), Victorian, Greek and mediaeval architecture. I step on the cobbled pavement until I'm in front of the Hippodrome theatre. I turn into a small side street with an employment agency on the corners just after a fancy-dress shop, with afro wigs in the window and a thunder bird's outfit on a mannequin with his hand on his hip in a 'camp' stance. My Gay friend would laugh at this. He doesn't call himself Gay, he just says he saw through the gender barrier and fell in love with an adult of the same sex. Him and his partner have a great relationship.

The street has an amusement arcade with a huge gold sign and gold coins, there are lit up signs in every window saying 'open'. The club is next door to the theatre with the double doors where people wait for autographs from their favourite actors. The club is painted black and all the windows have been replaced with mirrors. There are simple silver letters spelling out the name of the club on a sign protruding out from the front of the building, under this is a sentence in smaller letters saying 'one of the U.K's leading tabletop dancing clubs'. The sign is modestly understated and classy, I could walk in mistakenly thinking it was an upmarket wine bar. Across the road is an Italian restaurant and next to this is a tattoo removal shop, and next to that an Irish pub. These respectable businesses surrounding the club validated the place.

I'd never been to a lap dancing club before. I ring the bell by the front door and a big man dressed in a black suit appears. It's around lunch time and he has a bacon sandwich, he obviously isn't on shift yet.

'Can I speak to the manager please?' I ask nervously.

'Is he expecting you?' he stares at me and there's a glimmer of recognition.

'Yes,' I lied.

He lets me in and leads me through into a small room with a cloak room and a till and TV monitors that show the outside of the cub, behind a raised counter and through another door, down some wooden stairs and into a bigger room. I take in my surroundings. The club is modern with leather chairs around beech wood effect table tops with silver legs. The walls have framed photographs of women in provocative poses on them and are lit up, one wall has an American-diner-style seating area, with fancy blue lighting along the seats, projecting fanned out light onto the wall.

There's also a traditional ambience to this place because of the wooden furniture and leather chairs. The carpet is patterned red and the ceiling is a dusky purple colour, which makes the club appear enclosed, mirrors on the walls help to open the place up. It's warm; I imagine this is due to the women walking around virtually naked. I suppose it's nice to celebrate the female figure. The room has a beam in the middle due to a wall being removed and needing some support for the ceiling. At the end is a slightly raised stage with curtained doorways either side along the back wall, these feel like doors leading into bedrooms.

The decor gives off the impression of the club being exclusive. This is very different from the idea in my mind of a lap dancing club, I'd imagined somewhere seedy with the paint peeling off the walls and tacky decorations. The bar stretches down one side of the oblong room and is padded with leather. Lights are all the way along the bar, lighting up the black surface. Tables and chairs are in the middle of the room pointing in the direction of the stage. There are cocktail names on a blackboard on top of the bar and conveniently there are no price listings. The doorman takes me to the manager's office and knocks on the door. A dog starts barking.

'Shut up…. come in,' a gruff voice orders.

The security man holds the door open and I walk through. The room is dark, and it has posters and calendars of naked women on the walls, more celebration of the feminine figure. A man, in an expensive suit and well groomed, is sitting in a leather swivel chair. He's in his thirties and looks very confident and tough. The man gets up and goes over to his drink's cabinet, containing bottles of spirits, he pours himself out a drink. A Rottweiler is beside him. The man looks at us expectantly and directs his speech to his employee who's almost filling the whole doorway, no wonder he's in security.

The manager sips his drink and then asks, 'what is it?

'Sorry Boss, this lass wants to speak to you. She says you're expecting her.'

'Sorry to bother you,' I say, congenially, using my sweetest voice. 'I'm looking for work here.'

'What sort of work?' He asks, swirling his drink around in his expensive crystal glass. Then he looks keenly at me and asks, 'do I know you?'

'No, I-I think a dancer, I'm not sure.' I'm starting to lose my nerve; the Rottweiler is slobbering and keeps looking in my direction. 'I ask sir because it's important.' I try to sound as nice as possible.

He rises and opens the door for me, 'sorry I can't be more helpful,' and hearing the dog growling, I get up to depart his office quickly.

I then go back through the club and the security man lets me out onto the street. I manage to hold it together until the fresh air hits me and then burst into tears. I feel angry at myself for being weak, I should have asked more questions. I also feel deflated after the stuff I'd taken last night and the lack of sleep. I waited around for a while. If any staff arrive, I can speak to them about putting in a good word for me. I still feel shaken by the man's reaction to me; he wasn't very helpful.

I sit waiting for a while with my head in my hands, sitting on the pavement in the hope that a worker from the club will appear. I can't control my thoughts; I think about my partner. I wait for ages crying my eyes out. I'm sitting on the wall across the road, when eventually I see a woman approaching. She has a small-black-shoulder-bag with a gold chain strap and is clasping a pink wig in her hands. The woman's brushing it as she walks along. I make an educated guess that she works for the club. It is now about four o'clock.

'Excuse me, sorry to bother you, you dance at The Sweet House, don't you?' I say very politely.

The woman stops and looks at me confused. 'Do I know you?' she says, peering at me.

'No,' I reply.

'What do you want?' She asks and sounds annoyed. I notice her long-fake-gold-fingernails; they are disconcerting because they're like talons.

'I just need work in the club, preferably cash in hand,' I explain, 'I saw the boss earlier and he wasn't helpful.'

The woman's voice softens, she can probably see the streaky tear-tracks on my face; my eyeliner has probably run, 'come on Honey, let's go and get a coffee, I'm early anyway, I came in to sort my costume out, I ripped it last night, this is easily done when you're writhing around on a pole.' Becky smiles at me and I notice that she has an attractive face. Her makeup is flawless, almost making her look like a mannequin.

The woman starts to return the way she came, I follow, and she introduces herself; 'my name's Becky. What's your name?'

'Sara,' I reply, noticing how proficiently she walks in her high heels, they make her legs look long. For me, wearing shoes like that would be like walking on stilts. I feel plain next to Becky in my jeans, sweatshirt, and flat canvas shoes. I've always been a tomboy; I only dress feminine for events like meals in restaurants; maybe I should start to dress more ladylike. Becky stops in front of a café on the main street. We sit near the window. A Greek man comes over and takes our order of two cappuccinos. Becky pays. Becky reaches into her bag for a face wipe and leans over the table and dabs gently at my face.

'How do you know about the club?' she queries gently.

'My friend sent me, I need a job,' there's a hint of desperation in my voice. 'I've just arrived in Bristol. I really need some money. I am living in a squat.'

Becky ponders for a few seconds and then answers, 'I will speak to Drew, don't worry.' Becky shifts uneasily in her seat.

The drinks turn up and are placed in front of us and we both rip open the sugar sachets. You always need two sachets for one sugar, so this took a minute or two. It's funny how our sugar intake is limited if it costs businesses money.

'Becky, I just want a job. T-Bone sent me,' I explain. Becky's still looking uncomfortable and gazing out the window at the numerous people.

I thank Becky. My brain feels worn out. I feel like all my energy has drained away as if I'm a ghost of my former self. I sigh. Becky, seeing the tears in my eyes, gives me a sisterly hug to try to make me feel better.

'Come back to the club with me, Drew would let you work the bar and you could shadow me and learn how to dance, I could teach you the pole,' Becky smiles and adds, 'Drew may be dismissive but he knows you could make him money, you could save up for a deposit on a flat, once I have explained your situation, he can pay you in cash.'

I could see the sense in this, Becky was right, 'yeah, that would be good,' I answer.

'Right, let's go and see what we can do,' Becky says and puts her hands on my shoulders and propels me out of the door. We briskly walk back to the club and Becky rings the bell, when the security man opens the door, he raises his eyebrows when he sees me but doesn't utter a word. Becky marches me back to Drews office and knocks, upon hearing his command to enter, we do so. He's still sitting at his desk going through paperwork. Drew looks up with surprise.

'Drew, this is Sara and she needs some work desperately, she just arrived in Bristol,' Becky announces, 'I know you care about people,' Becky says this almost as if she is asking a question. 'She needs a job and I happen to know you need someone behind the bar and Sara would like me to train her up to dance. She is sofa surfing right now.' Becky has folded her arms together.

'Okay Becky, she's your responsibility though,' Drew replies in a gruff manner. He looks at me, 'come in on Tuesday at six o'clock and I will show you the ropes, wear a low-cut top and do your makeup,' Drew states, eyeing me up and down.

'Thank you, Sir,' I say, this was the perfect job to help me, Becky has made an ingenious suggestion.

'It's Drew,' Drew responds, 'now leave me alone,' he orders with a stern look.

When we get out into the corridor and shut the office door, I smile at Becky and she gives me another hug. I notice how long her eyelashes are.

'When you learn how to dance for people we could dance together,' Becky advises, 'we can make some good money, you will see Hun.'

I make my way back out and say goodbye to Becky at the door.

'I will see you Tuesday and I'll bring in a tight top for you,' Becky says, 'we are about the same size, I can do your hair and makeup too, just get here on time, Drew is big on punctuality,' she instructs me and waves as I wander off down the road, just before I turn, I looks back and see Becky stood smoking. I wave for the last time. Her lipstick smile stands out.

I decide to go and look for Squirrel and Innit, they may cheer me up. I go up past the theatre, the water features, and through the bus station, up, and past Jamaica street hostel with the people hanging out the front drinking or shouting out of the tiny windows. Evening is drawing in and I'm starting to feel a chill in the air. Gloucester road is busy, the pub garden is full, people are spilling out of The Canteen, and meet Squirrel on his begging spot. He is crossed legged on the floor with his cap out, sitting by the locked-up bikes. Street Drinkers are huddled in the music shop doorway across from him wrapped in duvets.

'Squirrel, have you seen Innit?' I ask.

'He's at the squat waiting for you,' he answers, 'go back and I'll return soon with some cans for us. Be careful of Kev,' Squirrel warns, 'Innit's been worried about you, he saw him today.' 'Cool Squirrel,' I reply and head back to the squat straight away.

Once up the steep hill, I knock on the orange door and Innit opens this for me and smiles a relieved smile. I join Mickey and Rene in the front room. They are all sat on the carpet around the pyramid, this looks surreal. Mickey is cooking up a hit for them, 'just in time,' he says, looking up at me.

'Where were you today?' Innit asks, 'Squirrel and I were worried; I have walked around looking for you three times. I got an amount of B's of T.J. to sell, I can keep us in Brown for a while,' he smiles.

'I went into the centre and found myself a job,' I state.

'Cool Sara, in it,' Innit grins, 'what are you gonna be doing?'

'I'm working behind the bar in a club called The Sweet House,' I

reply, redoing my ponytail. 'I've heard of that place,' Innit

announces, 'that's a lap dancing club, in it.'

'Yeah,' I answer.

'I'll walk you to work then,' Innit says and smiles a cheeky grin, 'I bet some fit women work there.'

I laugh. Innit walking me to and back from work would be helpful.

Rene pulls her skirt down and says, 'you can always come to work with me.'

'I will see how this goes. Thanks though.'

We all sit back and enjoy our hit. I feel peace. My pink-tinted sunglasses firmly on again and I feel out of this world.

Chapter Ten; The Lap Dancing Club

I have my first shift behind the bar at the club tonight. I spend time with Innit and Squirrel mooching about the centre. Then Innit walks me past the Hippodrome theatre and up to the club. I gaze at myself in the mirrored windows. I really hope Becky comes through on her promise of a top and doing my makeup. I see people in the window of the Italian restaurant, I would treat Innit and Squirrel to a meal there at some point. I feel excited in a strange way, this is going to be an experience. When I get to the door, I ring the bell and the same ginormous security man opens this. Innit stands beside me and looks slightly taken aback by the man's size. The man looks at Innit and opens the door to me. He puts out his arm to stop Innit entering.

'Innit, I'll see you at two am,' I say, 'please be on time and don't fall asleep.'

'Okay Sara,' he says obediently, peering at me with his lovely brown eyes, 'don't worry, just chill.'

'Bye mate,' Innit says to the security man and the man raises his eyes up to the sky.

I walk through the door with trepidation and go by the counter with the till and monitors, past the cloakroom, and down to the main room. Drew is standing with Becky behind the bar, they both smile as I enter which is reassuring.

'Well done Hun,' Becky says, 'I was worried you weren't going to turn up and I had come in early for nothing,' Becky is flawlessly made up again, she must be a makeup expert, she could make a good beautician.

Drew is in a suit again; he has smartly cut dark hair and is clean shaven and you can tell he is the proprietor of the club. He and Becky are having a drink.

'Sara, I'm busy so I'm going to get Becky to show you the ropes, she volunteered her services, she must like you,' he comes out from behind the bar to stand beside me and puts a hand on my shoulder, 'don't get nervous, tonight is a slow night and you are extra, tonight is just a training experience, Becky started work here on the bar, when you finish, come and see me in the office and I will pay you,' he walks off briskly without waiting for a response.

I turn to Becky and grin, 'thanks Becky, did you bring me a top?'

'Yep, you will be making mega tips with the top I have brought you,' she smiles, 'chat to the customers because they tip better then and if anyone tries to grab you or makes you feel uncomfortable in anyway, speak to Tony the security man, he will have a word with them, the men can get a bit grabby when they have had a few.'

'Thanks,' I say.

'Put your bag behind the bar for now and I will show you the lockers in a bit,' she says.

Becky goes through all the drinks and prices and shows me how to make the cocktails, and where the storeroom is, my head starts to spin. When she has run through everything and shown me how to ring all the drinks up, she then asks me which drink I would like and I ask for a coke with lemon which I pour out myself.

'We are going to have a break before people start coming in, you can get ready and meet some of the other dancers,' Becky beckons me to follow with her finger and we go out to a room around the back that looks like a dressing room, covered in mirrors, with hair straighteners and make up. Lockers stretch down the side wall.

'Put your bag in there and remember to lock it,' she says, 'don't lose the key.'

I do as she says, and we go and sit together in front of the mirrored wall. Becky reaches in her bag and produces a red top for me to change into, which I do, and then proceeds to do my hair and makeup, she glues some false eyelashes on my eyelids and shades in my eyes, the makeup she does is heavier than I have ever worn, the black eyeliner is applied very thickly, I don't recognise myself. Becky then plaits my small plaits into a big plait down one side of my head which looks stylish.

'I knew you would scrub up well,' she smiles.

Becky starts to put on a blue wig in the shape of a bob with a fringe, she also takes off her jeans and top and is wearing a gold, skimpy one-piece swimsuit with a G-string. She grabs some extra high heels out of her bag and leaves them on the floor ready for her to adorn when the time is right. Becky has a great body and is confident, she pulls the outfit off well. We hear chatter as three more women enter and start to off load their bags into the lockers, slamming the doors shut. They are laughing about something.

'Hi,' Becky calls over to them as they start to get ready, 'this is our new bar person, Sara,' and all three women look around curiously. Becky turns back to me and says, 'these are three of our dancers, Jody, Carissa, and Poppy.'

Two of the women smile and one of the women, called Poppy, walks over to us. 'Hi, nice to meet you.' Poppy is curvaceous and has curly long blonde hair, her face is plain and without makeup.

Poppy rubs my shoulder, 'plaster on a smile, we are going to make some money,' Poppy gets out her phone and Bluetooth speaker and puts on the tune by M.I.A Paper Planes. She starts singing along as she does her makeup and transforms. When this is completed, she turns to Becky, 'if anyone asks for a private dance off two girls can I pair with you tonight?'

'Yeah, we will need to practice,' Becky grins, 'I am meant to be showing Sara the ropes, let's do her a performance, she can tell us what looks good.'

Poppy searches for a song on her phone and presses play, the beats start and Poppy and Becky stand in front of me in their skimpy clothes. They start to dance together, making me laugh because of the clown-like looks on their faces.

'Obviously, we will be looking sexy when we do this for real,' Poppy says.

They both start to swing their hair around in a circle and stand with their backs to me gyrating their asses, this is comical. They then both drop their heads to the floor and grasp their legs with their hands and I can see their upside-down faces, smiling in-between their legs. They pop their heads up again and start dancing to the beats together, Poppy sweeps Becky's hair back out of her face and runs her finger down her shoulder and under her bra strap. Becky turns around and Poppy undoes the top. Becky holds this over her breasts whilst Poppy undoes her strap and does the same. Then they both turn to face me and drop their bra tops to the floor. They are standing naked from the waist up, breasts exposed. Then they face each other and stand together, and Poppy sucks her fingers seductively and tweaks Becky's nipple. Becky runs her hand down her face to her navel and then cups Poppy's breasts in her hands and lowers her head and licks up the middle until she comes to face Poppy and they full on snog each other, almost forgetting that I am there. Then they stop as the tune finishes and turn to face me. I am stunned.

'What do you think Sara?' Becky asks.

'Erm…good,' I say.

Poppy and Becky start laughing, 'she's speechless,' Poppy says. 'Watch us on the pole, Becky is one of the best pole dancers in here,' Poppy enlightens me.

'I do it for a circus group in a club, we have fire dancers and people doing aerial hoops. I like doing this a lot better than here, but I need the money,' Becky reveals and plonks down on the chair next to me. 'I said I would show you some moves on the pole, there is a real skill to it, similar to the circus act where they use material to do acrobatics. Come, we need to start to make a move out into the main room, start milling about, Carissa do you fancy starting on the pole.'

'Yeah that's fine Becky,' Carissa says in her silver bikini.

I wander out with them and make my way behind the bar, glancing round at the people in the club with interest. They are 'normal' people, some office workers and others on a night out in groups. Some of the groups include women and everyone seems to be having a laugh. I wait behind the bar, watching and pouring drinks.

The women socialise whilst virtually naked and I try not to look, this is a strange environment. I do as Becky says and watch the pole dancers. They look beautiful. They are trying to be sexy which spoils the performance a little but when they are doing moves on the pole, climbing up it and twirling down and holding various poses, they look amazing, pole dancing is actually an artform. I can see why this is linked with circus skills.

A man sits down at the bar and instigates a conversation with me, 'your new here aren't you?' he asks.

'Yeah, I have just started,' I reply.

The man is smart and casual, but you can tell he has money by the cut of his clothes, he has on a good watch. I start to play with my side plait, trying to look appealing.

'Yeah,' the man smiles, 'good to meet you, here's a tip.' He puts a ten-pound note in my hand and then gets up and goes and sits around the stage to watch the dancers.

I can't wait for the shift to be over; this can't come soon enough. I clean up and go through to Drew's office and collect my pay, I have made some decent tips. Then I leave the club, waving goodbye to Becky and the other women. Innit isn't there so I wait. The night is dark, and I can hear the drone of the traffic. The club is slightly secluded; the alleyway is small and off the beaten track. A man wanders by and stares at me in my makeup and tight top and he grabs my ass.

'You're one of those dancers from the club,' he says, I can smell the alcohol on his breath. 'No contact, well I am touching now aren't I,' he says and pushes me up against the club window.

Just then Becky comes out, with a wine bottle in hand, and Innit turns into the alleyway.

'Fuck off,' she says and pulls the guy off me brandishing the bottle. Innit runs up and pushes the man away from me. The man runs off.

'Sara, don't go out of the club alone,' Becky advises, looking upset, 'some of the sleazeball men hang around waiting to catch us off guard, some are nice and just want to take us out and others aren't so nice.'

'Innit was supposed to be here waiting for me,' I explained.

'I was late by five minutes, sorry, in it,' he says, looking guilty.

'Innit, is that your name?' Becky asks.

'Yes, in it.'

'Ring the bell and I'll make the doorman let you in to wait upstairs,' Becky says, looking concerned.

'Thanks Becky,' I responded.

'Don't mention it, some clubs pay for a taxi when women have to work to the early hours but Drew isn't going to do that, the least he can do is let Innit wait inside,' Becky smiles at me, 'he is just a disgruntled customer who was probably asked to leave because he got too hands on.' Becky has on normal clothes and looks different. She still has on her high heels. 'You are scary, were you going to hit him with the bottle you have in your hand?' I ask.

'I am just waiting to be picked up by my partner, but I saw you coming out and was worried as to how you were getting home, and I wanted to give you this bottle of wine, perks of the job, thank god I came out,' Becky sighs. 'I am going to go and wait in the club and have a drink with Drew, I have to keep him happy as he is the boss,' Becky states, 'you did well tonight Sara, okay. Drew forgot to say that he would like you to come in next Thursday. This weekend we are okay because the person you are replacing is leaving next week.'

'Okay Becky, thanks for all your help,' I reply, 'you are a legend and you are amazing on the pole, I loved watching you.'

'Told you, that will be you in a few months' time,' Becky exclaims.

I laugh. I couldn't see that happening somehow. Innit and I stroll through the streets to get back to the squat, passing the twenty-four-hour shop with people outside. This place is dubious at this time and I am glad Innit is with me, shadowy people hang around as if they are about to jump out on you and take you for what you have. Gloucester road is nosey and busy, the clubs and bars are open, and lines of people are outside either waiting to get in or getting air with pint glasses in hand. I am glad there are people around, not just the scavengers.

We go down Picton street and up Richmond road and we sit and chat for a while, Squirrel joins us. I produce my bottle of wine and share this around. I tell Squirrel about the guy outside the club and this makes him angry.

'Sara, you need to be careful in Bristol,' he advises, 'this is a city, you need to be aware,' Squirrel announces reticently, he has black rings under his eyes and is looking worn out, he still has on the same clothes and his dreadlocks are still all over the place which makes me smile.

I'm tired and fall asleep on the lounge floor, the pyramid is starting to crumble, and the bits are covering the floor, we would have to clear this up soon. Innit wakes me and sends me upstairs. Squirrel says goodnight. Innit follows me into his room, his stuff is in there and we are too tired to move this. We both crawl into our sleeping bags and lie down beside each other. Innit kisses me lightly on the cheek. I'm now a working woman with a roof over my head, things are looking up in Bristol, and I am in the ideal place to gather insight, I have learnt loads already. I still feel the ache in the pit of my stomach about my partner.

Innit puts his head on his hand and says, 'I have saved us a hit each, just H, sorry, I did all the W in with Mickey whilst you were at work, in it,' he sits up and gets his spoon out and starts to cook our hits.

When he is finished, he gets me after a few failed attempts, I now have painful places on my arm, and I feel the familiar warm feeling engulf my body and lie back with Innit's arm around me and my pink-tinted sunglasses on and my mind feels peace and comfort, Hurt and anxiety fade. I AM IN A BEAUTIFUL PERFECT WORLD WERE THERE ARE NO MONSTERS. I AM IN A DREAM WORLD. LIVING THE DREAM. I AM LIVING THE FAIRY-TALE.

Nightmare Two; The Reinterpreted Fairy-Tale 'Hansel and Gretel' by The Brothers Grimm (1812)

After what seemed like no time, I woke up again. I rub my eyes and grab my top and pull it over my head. I sit up and look around my new room. The walls are pink with miniature fairies balancing on flowers and branches... I hadn't noticed the branches before. These are growing from evenly spaced trees all around the wallpaper. I see roots of trees sprouting out of the skirting boards.

As I look down, my pink-tinted sunglasses slip off my nose, I haven't even realised that I'm wearing them. I pick them up and place them in my pocket, bemused. Staring back at the walls, the candy pink background is now dark grey. The fairies have disappeared and all that remains are the trees. I suddenly feel a chill in the air. I shake my sleeping bag to the floor and step out. Rather disconcertingly, the floor crunches underneath my feet and I feel the uneven surface below. I glance down and notice the ground is covered in multiple layers of leaves and twigs.

The room starts to spin, and I look around me bewildered. The trees on the wallpaper are now three-dimensional and real. I can smell the real musty pine smell of a forest. I walk over and feel the rough bark beneath my fingertips. The bark appears black and the branches look like knobbly witches' hands scrabbling at the night sky.

As I raise my head, I see the full moon shining downward and producing shadows merging into creatures of the forest. Eyes are everywhere, like wolves waiting to pounce and strip the flesh from my bones. I start to panic and stumble around, hearing the noise of my footsteps in the silence, except for the bird calls. I stumble over a tree's upturned roots and roll over, twigs and leaves attaching to my clothes and hair. I'm aware of a dark presence. Hello Darkness My Old Friend.

I hear crackling. Then, orange and yellow light flickers in the night, thawing the chill. There's a bonfire. I get up and walk over to the big fire, which is burning fiercely, stacked skilfully. The heat's comforting. I sit mesmerised, gazing into the heart of the fire, seeing little orange glow worms wriggling across the wood. I inhale the smoke as it rises.

As I turn away from the intense heat, a face floats into view, distorted by shadow. I rub my eyes again, blinking a couple of times to make the face more lucid. The appearance alters, developing into a mirror and I see my own face

Innit reappears beside me. 'Come on, we have to go home to find Squirrel,' he says and starts to lead the way, taking my hand. I feel the touch of his skin which is as light as air. He pulls me along and birds start their dawn chorus as the sky lightens. Then Innit starts digging at the brass and copper coloured floor. 'I've discovered the trail I left for us… we can find our way now,' he says with enthusiasm. I look down and notice little white pebbles leading away from us. We follow them, pulling back the bushes and branches where we need to.

I see that one of the tiny pebbles shines in the sun like a polished gemstone. I let go of his hand and pick it up. The pebble is smooth and soft to touch, my nail makes an impression on the surface. I spot a transparent skin peeling off the pebble and pull at this. The thin layer unravels, and I realise this is cling film. The pebble's in fact are balls of cling film.

Innit is calling me; 'come on, we have to locate Squirrel.'

Again, following the trail, I start to notice a large shape looming ahead. This becomes clearer the closer we come and develops into a building, The Sweet House. He runs to the door and goes through, closing it behind him. I follow, and when I reach the door, I try to pull it open. The door remains shut.

There's a metal knocker in the shape of Drew's head, the owner of the club. I knock the metal door knocker and the sound reverberates around. Everything vibrated with the sound. This is like a loud continuous beat of a tribal drum and makes my heart skip.

The drumbeats carry on and become a techno tune; speeding up until it's just one constant sound and then disappears into silence.

I place my hands against the door, and they start to sink into the wooden surface which has become sticky and pliable. I push my body through and fall through on to the other side, having to pull the strings of this sticky material off me. It's like I'm escaping from a spider's web. I tug the fibrous gel off me, wiping my mouth to be able to breathe like a baby that's just been born.

Suddenly the substance is like liquid mercury, and solidifies, dropping to the floor. I'm inside the club and walk through the corridor to Drew's open office door. Inside, I see Drew in front of a dog cage containing me as a little girl. Drew opens the cage door and throws in a severed finger. The little girl looks thin and starts to tear bits off with her teeth, blood dripping down her face as the finger bone appears.

I head out and into the main room of the club in disgust. I need to find Becky and tell her that Drew's in his office. I notice Innit on the small raised stage acting out a scene of a play, and run over to him; the two poles used by the female dancers have disappeared. Two women, one I recognise as Becky, are on the stage dressed up in clothes of the medieval era. They're all talking in the Old English language of Shakespeare; 'What will these hands ne'er be clean...' I wish I'd paid more attention to my English Literature A Level.

I start trying to call out to Innit, but my words won't come out. I can't speak. I try to clamber up onto the stage but can't, the stage is surrounded by a thick transparent bubble. I try to burst it. I pick up a champagne bottle off of one of the tables surrounding the stage and throw this as hard as I can at the bubble; it bounces off and almost strikes me.

The bottle lands and smashes into smithereens, the pieces glint like emeralds covering the floor around the chairs. The neck of the bottle has remained intact and is jagged at the end. I pick this up and try to tear through the bubble but it's impossible, like trying to get through a plate of thick steel. I pick up a stool from in front of the bar and throw it and this just rebounds and smashes into a table, knocking the furniture across the floor. I am confused by this.

I then turn back to the stage and see Innit with a giant syringe shaped gun to his head. I scream; 'Innit... 'NO.'

Innit eyes stare at me with a vacant look. A deafening, echoing, shot rings out. Evil Echoes. The bubble turns into drops of rain which pours onto the stage. I see Innit's body slump to the floor. I step up onto the stage and run over to him, cradling his body and rocking back and forth as the blood seeps out of the side of his head. The bright red blood is running into a pool and this unexpectedly changes into the colour pink.

As I sit there, the club fades away, and I'm back out in the open forest with the early morning sun flashing through the trees. As I kneel, hugging Innit, the breeze is blowing my plaited hair in front of my face. As I push my hair behind my ears, I feel Innit's body lighten and look down. He's become a skeleton, just bones and a skull.

I can see that the forest floor is covered in images of my dead partner with pink eyes. The ground appears as if it's made of rubber and he's trying to break out, his face, hands and feet stretching this in places. I scream and look back at Innit's bones; they turn into snow which starts to fall from the sky and covers the forest floor. As I put out my hand and catch the snowflakes, like sand, I observe that each one is a perfect unique pattern and beautiful.

Suddenly, I'm in my room wrapped up in my sleeping bag covered in sweat and trembling. I sit up, trying to recover my composure, looking around me to verify whether I'm really in my room. I want a real home. Maybe the ghost of my dead partner might have been communicating with me from the grave. Even my dream world isn't safe for me anymore.

I listen for Innit's breathing. For a split second, I think I can't hear any and then he moves slightly. I snuggle up to Innit and his warmth soothes me. He moulds around me in his sleep and my head fits into the crook of his neck. His arm rests on my body in a loose hug. Thankfully, he is present. I continue to listen to his breathing in the twilight. There are no curtains upstairs and the room is lit by the light from the streetlamps. This light creates shadows in the room from the lager cans on the windowsill. I doze off again. The nightmare I had was unsettling, but I chalk it down to nerves about starting my new job.

Chapter Eleven; The Dragon

Innit wants to find Mickey when we wake. He is in The Bear Pit as usual. I am feeling rubbish, my eyes are watering and I'm getting recurring cramps and feeling cold. Innit keeps giving me a knowing look, as if to say I told you so. We walk along the busy road past the bakery and music shop, bus stop, and down the steps. I don't really notice much because I feel ill.

'Innit, safe Bruv,' they touch fists. Mickey sneezes five times. 'Clucking Bruv, went into the centre to beg up some money and the police have been following me around, they arrested me and took me to the police station and I had to be processed whilst clucking Bruv, fucking shit. I can't even spit any lyrics, Bruv, going to be sick.'

'Why are they on your back so much Bruv, in it?' Innit asks.

'Someone's been robbing up the shops Bruv, they think it's me,' Mickey answers.

'And is it, in it?' Innit responds.

'That would be telling Bruv,' Mickey smiles a huge grin and laughs, 'what do they expect, I'm a heroin addict.' Mickey spins his baseball cap around on his head.

Innit laughs.

'Keep your head down, I can sort you out now, I have a job for you later, knock about with us today and come and stay in the squat tonight,' he states.

We say goodbye to everyone, and Mickey joins us for the day.

'We need to score Bruv, who's on?'

'JT will be on Bruv, how much are you getting?' Mickey asks.

'I wanna get three W, I have B myself to sell, in it,' Innit responds.

'Use my phone Bruv,' Mickey hands him his smartphone.

Innit looks surprised, 'where did you get this?'

'Robbed it off a table in The Canteen last night,' he laughs, 'it's their fault, they shouldn't be so fucking stupid, Bruv, it's still got credit on Bruv, hurry up, they might block it soon Bruv,' Mickey explains.

Innit phones the dealer and we all go to meet him.

I walk beside Innit as we go up the steps of The Bear pit, past the billboards at eye level, and up towards Gloucester road, through the massive Holiday Inn building, with slits for windows, which creates a tunnel for the road to go under, and past the giant mushroom and golden sun sign, across from us, a man is sitting holding his sleeping bag with his friend drinking a can of Strongbow. A man is sitting up the road in his wheelchair with no legs. We pass the turning down to Circlomedia and can see the spire along with a massive yellow crane, and The Bike Project across the road, with the metal wheel sculptures and a seagull passing overhead. And turn in along the road, passing the lime green bushes, and cross to stand by the flats.

A man cycles by on a bike. Innit walks across the road in pursuit, down the street, and then casually walks up to us as if he is taking a leisurely stroll.

'Come on Innit, I'm clucking Bruv,' Mickey says and starts to sneeze again, then is almost sick.

'Sorry Bruv, you have to be careful round here, JT just told me he's being watched, and he got stopped and searched the other day, in it' Innit explains. 'Sara, you're quiet today, are you okay, in it?' Innit asks.

'I just want to get high, Innit, I don't feel like talking,' I responded.

Innit puts his arm around me, 'everything is going to be okay, in it, we're gonna have a Snowball to share.'

I don't reply. Mickey and Innit and I walk up past the mattress and bins and recycle bins full of beer bottles. Seeing two pigeons with shiny purple and green necks. Then we go past the newsagents. I am starting to feel better. Moving around helps slightly, I am cold, I know that.

Innit walks me some of the way down the alleyway and then absconds with Mickey. I'm not enjoying myself. I wish I could get Innit around some clean people, just not liking the desperate characters I'm meeting. Well, hopefully I can leave soon and go back to my normal life when I have a secure address.

Unhappily, I go up the alley to wait for them, walking past another giant piece of graffiti covering a house, and wait. Sitting on the curved paving where the road joins the alley. The sky is light, the roof tops and aerials reach up into the blue and white clouds, and no one else is around. Across from me is a red sign saying that the road is closed, which is funny because it isn't a road, there's a garage behind it. There are delicate-purple-bellflowers poking out from the moss and plants, trying to grow through at the sides of the concrete.

I study the double yellow lines which curve around underneath me and finish where the alley starts, a CND sign has been painted on the road, I'd signed one of their petitions once for nuclear disarmament, my mum had been angry and said we needed nuclear weapons. I can't see why. The alien invasion probably, as if that's going to happen. A sign on the house opposite me says 'vote green'. Green is one of my favourite colours, and I love nature and animals, so I'd vote for this party, you could call me an idealist. There are scribbled names everywhere in green, blue and purple. The sun shines off the surface of one of the houses. As I sit, I study everything. There's an iron gate made up of conjoined squares with a trellis behind it, ivy grows covering every inch, giving flawless privacy, which makes me wonder as to whether the plant is real. On the side of the wall are the words 'BARKING BABYLON WOOF' this befuddles me.

The alley is tarmacked unevenly, obviously parts were done at different times, some bits smooth and some gravel and stones. I hear a noise like a band saw and see a bright yellow helicopter above my head. I lean my head on my hand and close my eyes, listening to the traffic sounds in the distance. I sit wondering where Innit is and how long he will be, considering whether I should return to the squat. Then I hear the crunching noise of footsteps and look up to see a postman pushing his trolley full of mail along the alley. I go back to studying the graffiti opposite.

Hearing footsteps again, I assume the postman is back. I don't look up until I realise they're getting close. A figure's walking up the alleyway. His hood's up, and he's walking in a strange jerking manner which worries me. I decide to remain where I am until he has passed. I'm near houses after all and the alleyway is visible to them. My hand grabs my Rape Alarm. I still feel like I'm not properly in the reality of here and now. He gets nearer and I can see the sports motif on his dark blue sweatshirt. His trainers are dirty. He was smart and clean the first time I met him.

He weirdly shuffles along and is remarkably close to me now. I sit silently, hoping he will pass me by promptly. His face is obscured by his hood. The part I can see is pale. We're within an arm's length of each other. He stops and turns to face me. My heart sinks. It is Kev, the Chav from the park who attacked Innit with a knife. He looks at me and his face is contorted, the irises have red around. He has a peculiar look in his eyes. A vacant dead look. I'm not going to be able to escape and I have sucked in the air, petrified, I can't move, I can't speak, I'm stuck to the floor, I've never seen anyone look so weird and hopefully never will again; he looks like the undead in films. I press the button on my Alarm, the sound admitted is horrible. He grabs the Alarm and throws it against the wall, it breaks and the horrendous sound fades into nothing.

I try to escape and rise from the low wall, shaking, I've no idea what's going to happen. Kev reaches out and grabs me by the shoulders with his dirty hands. He pushes me down onto the floor, banging my head on the concrete so hard that my vision goes yellow. *Of all the colours, why yellow*? Pink would be an improvement. I can feel the pain. He grips my legs as I thrash around. He smells like dead air.

Kev growls like a dog, 'Grr...rrr...rrr. You Bitch, INNIT'S BITCH,' he shouts and punches me in the face, his punch hurts.

I feel the heat and pain in my face as it swells up, tasting the iron in my blood. I'm in shock.
He then pulls his trousers down. I stay motionless because I don't want to be struck again. If I let him do what he wants then maybe I'll be allowed to live, I shut my eyes. Numb. If I don't move or speak, maybe I'm not here. I'm out of my body, looking down on myself and see the back of his hooded head and body, the grey ass, with skin hanging off in places, he is straddling my body on the floor.

Kev compresses my throat with his hand, holding me down and I open my eyes and find myself looking into his red tinged dead eyes. I notice that his hair is patchy in places underneath the hood. He looks vacant, dead and soulless. He unbuttons my trousers and pulls them down to my knees.

 I feel the cold on my legs. And then I feel the cold hard thing stabbing in between my legs, until it goes in and out, like a strike to the heart. He's vigorously thrusting in and out, each time his face gets closer to me, with each inward thrust, and I close my eyes. It feels like I'm on a fair ride, when the ride is spinning around, and I feel the anxiety because the ride is about to pull in another direction, straining each nut and bolt, not knowing whether I'm going to spin into oblivion and certain death. The cold rugged hand is gripping my throat and tightens when I move, I stay still and rigid and dry, so dry that each banging thrust hurts. He smells like dead air.

 'GRRRRR….' I hear.

 The tears drip from my cheeks. I look up to the sky. There is nothing I can do. I'm helpless.

 'Grrrr…' I hear.

 Then there's a last thrust and I hear a gurgling sound, like a dog being suffocated. I feel the cold stabbing thing pull out and glutinous gunge spurts onto my leg, like grainy half zombie slime. Kev looks down and pulls his foreskin back, like he's wringing out a wet smelly sock and flicks the last remaining stuff off his hand at me; as if he's shaking off something unpleasant like a bogie. I grasp onto the concrete and gravel, grazing my fingers in the process. I push myself up and away from him. His stranglehold has gone and he's now pulling up his tracksuit bottoms. He kicks me in the side. I see his foot aiming for me and brace for impact, the feeling's hard to describe. It's like a nervous cloud in my mind until the impact comes, and I feel the pain. I think he's cracked my ribs. Then I notice Innit coming into view. Still numb.

 'Sara, get out of the way, in it.' He looks livid.

I try to muster up the will to move. This is hard for me. Innit roundhouse kicks Kev in the chest and knocks him off his feet and sends him over onto the floor. His trousers fall back down. His half erect appendage is like a warty, hanging hybrid slug. His hood has fallen, and his hair is sticking up all over the place in clumps. He has cuts and grazes down the side of his face and gravel stuck in the wounds.

'Innit you CUNT, GR...'

Innit heaves me up with his bandaged hand, his lovely brown eyes and face peering at me in concern. I'm hysterical. Innit's pulling me down the alley at high speed. I see Kev getting up and toppling over again. His trousers are around his ankles. He starts to pull them up. I've pulled mine up and have disgusting sticky goo on the side of my hand. We're running as fast as we can, panting, around and up to the squat. Tears continue to fall like rivers out of my eyes. I'm sick. When we arrive at the squat, Innit opens the orange door gently and we almost fall through. Innit shuts the door quietly behind us and grabs my hand.

'Come, let's get you cleaned up, in it.'

He puts his arm around my shoulders and guides me up the stairs, walking behind me. He takes my hand again at the top of the stairs and leads me into the bathroom, there he removes his sweatshirt and pulls his T-shirt over his head and a half naked Innit places me down on the side of the bath. He runs hot water in the sink and adds some liquid soap until the water is lathery and I can smell the fragrance. He soaks his T-shirt and adds more soap.

'Sara, I'm just gonna wash you,' he says, kissing the side of my face lightly.

My trousers are still undone so he gets me to stand up and edges them down slightly and starts to wash the slime off my leg, switching between hands so his bandage doesn't get too wet. Washing me like an old lady or like how Mary Magdalene washed

Jesus's feet in The Bible. He is gentle and fastidious. He then pulls them up for me gently. I'm quiet, still in shock. When he has finished washing my face, which throbs as he does so, he starts to wash my hands. Then he runs me a bath of hot water and fills it with liquid soap so the bubbles lather into foam. He grabs some black leggings for me from his room.

 'I was gonna give these to you, I found them on a wall down the road, they look brand new,' he says, looking worried and upset. 'I'll go in the other room whilst you have a bath and get changed, in it.'

 I get in the tub and wash myself robotically, cleaning inside myself thoroughly. I stand in front of the bathroom mirror for ten minutes, not able to move. I hear Innit knocking so I ease into the leggings, leaving the jeans scrunched up on the floor, and drift in a daze into the hallway where Innit waits nervously smoking. He has put on his sweatshirt. I drift into my pink room with fairy wallpaper and Innit follows.

 Quietly, Innit gets out his pipe, sneezing three times whilst doing so. Innit's body is lacking heroin. He then opens the tiny ball of Cling film and opens it onto a crushed can which he has got from the front room. Innit has halved the stuff as accurately as possible and is loading up his asthma inhaler pipe, with pin pricked tin foil on the end to place the ash on that he has collected. Once the pipe is loaded, he passes this to me. This must be bad because Innit would always go first.

 'Thank you,' I say profoundly and Innit lights the end for me as I inhale. I exhale and feel the high engulfing me. I feel better. I can't feel the pain quite as much.

 Innit takes the pipe, rubbing my shoulder and does the same. I push the glasses back down onto my face and see the usual pink cloud exhaled from him. I still can't really talk, and my mouth has gone numb from the stuff making this even harder. I'm sitting in my fairy land after being raped by a half zombie. The stuff has taken effect, I feel numb. I get out my figurative sunglasses and place them on. My view turns a shade of pink. Innit wretches after his pipe and staggers into the bathroom where I hear him vomit.

He comes back in after washing out his mouth and *cooks up his hit.*

'Can you do me one Innit please?' I ask, 'I need one after what just happened.'

'Sara, you can't get a habit,' Innit orders, 'I will do you one now, I saved some crack and am having a snowball, which is both H and W,' Innit replies, 'the buzz is amazing.'

Innit cooks up the heroin and when this has cooled down, crushes the white powder of the crack into the spoon and he pulls up twenty mils for me in a syringe. Innit jabs his needle into his veins desperately until the familiar red appears and he pushes the liquid in, and his face goes back to being comfortably vacant. When he is coherent enough, I pull up my top and allow him to tie the shoelace around my arm, he gets a vein straight away and carefully pushes the contents into my arm. I sit back and wait for the buzz. This comes swiftly. I get the nice mellow feel of the H but also the high from the cocaine, my mind drifts into nothingness and then is suddenly alert and drifting and alert. One minute I am on a pink cloud and then it feels like warm summer rain is waking me up. I feel tip top, brand new, out of this world, everything that has just happened melts away into nothingness. My head is between my legs and falls to the floor, my symbolic sunglasses pushing against my face. My forehead is on the floor and I don't care, I can't feel the floor, all I feel is this amazing tide of calm and relaxation, an all-encompassing pleasurable feeling that is hard to describe.

We come round a couple of hours later. Innit is led down on my sleeping mat in a foetal position and he places his hands over his eyes as if in inner turmoil. I move over towards him and pull one of his hands over me in a half hug whilst lying next to him, my view now being of the pink ceiling.

'Sara, I am so sorry, in it,' he says, peering sideways at me, his head now up on his hand. His pupils are like pin holes.

I pull his bandaged hand, which is hugging me, onto my heart and then down to touch my nipple and up to my mouth. He circles my lips with his butterfly touch and I gently suck his fingers, playing with them with my tongue. I just want to replace that awful memory with something better. Whilst sucking his fingers with my eyes closed, I then feel a licking around my lips and gently pushing into my mouth, playing with my tongue gently at first, and then forceful, pushing deep into my mouth.

My eyes are closed and Innit kisses my ear gently and whispers, 'are you okay Sara, are you sure this is what you want?'

I pull his hand down and place it between my legs and he starts to play. Trying to find the right spot until he finds it. He pulls my sunglasses off and slings them to my side. I grasp at them and hold them tight.

'Ah…' the word escapes from my mouth, 'ah…'

My skin is tingling, he is licking and kissing my nipples, 'ah…'

He's working fast with his fingers and then spits on one and starts to push it inside me. He bites my nipple and I feel pain, sharp and luscious over the top of that tingling feeling. I feel the mental release as I'm about to orgasm but Innit stops and pulls down his trousers and touches himself to make himself harder and then gently turns me over and is inside me as I face the ground. Then he turns me back around and I orgasm and so does he. He pulls out and cum squirts onto my tummy and breasts; when finished, he rubs this into me lovingly. We lay down. I feel happier.

Innit gets out some medication from his pocket, 'take one of these, Jay gave them to me. They are sleeping tablets called Zanex,' Innit says and offers me a long white pill. 'They will make you sleep, crush it up in your mouth.'

I take the pill.

Nightmare Three; The Reinterpreted Fairy-Tale 'Little Red Riding Hood'.

I woke up early in my home near Camberley. Confused, I cross the landing, confused, and go downstairs. Had I just dreamed of living in Bristol? I walk through the hall, past the oak dresser, and into the kitchen. I see my mother making breakfast and we sit at the table. She has made toast for me. I realise that I'm sitting in the Pyjamas that I used to wear last year. I'm very confused. Had I just had an epic dream?

'Can you go and visit Mathew in hospital,' my mother asks.

'Why is Mathew in the hospital mum? I query.

My mum looks at me quizzically, 'what's wrong with you today? He's in hospital because he's ill of course,' my mum informs me. 'He is on the ward, Scarlet.'

'Oh, yeah,' I reply.

'Don't say you're losing your mind as well, they say mental health problems run in families and your grandmother was hospitalised,' my mum comes over to me and gives me a hug.
'Are you okay?'

'I'm fine mum, just disorientated, had a strange lucid dream last night,' I reply. 'I would love to see Mathew. I'll get dressed and go immediately.'

My mother stands beside me as I munch my toast, 'I will drop you halfway and then you'll have to walk, don't stray from the path okay,' she says. My mother hands me a red box, 'take this with you, there are a few of his favourite things inside, I have put in his Bible, when I drop you off, don't stray from the path,' she says and picks up her cup of tea and heads up to her room.

  The kettle is bubbling away. I make myself tea with one sugar and then I go up to my room. My room is how it was a years ago, my photographs of myself and my partner Mathew up on my notice board, my list of universities too. My laptop is on my desk ready. Books are everywhere, piled up on the floor, this is the only mess in my otherwise pristine room. My room's plain white and I love it. Some of my Mathew's paintings are framed and up on my wall. There's a painting of us together in reds, pinks, yellows, and oranges; Mathew is a talented artist.

  I open my pine wardrobe and am met with rows of shoes. I start to take out some clothes. My favourite burgundy poncho is there, with the big hood, my favourite long red jumper with the slits down the side which could almost be worn as a dress. Today I'll dress comfortably. I sit in front of my mirror and get out my expensive makeup. I love makeup. Good makeup. The stuff that doesn't clog up your pores, I use a moisturiser and sunscreen, and then foundation. I've eye shadow in all colours, like the rainbow, I put a base on my eyelids to keep the eye shadow on once applied and black eyeliner, you can't go anywhere without it. I pencil in my eyebrows with brown powder. I use my tinted lip balm. I dress in some smart black trousers and a smart cream top. I push my arms through the side holes in the poncho and pull it over my head. I can hide when my hood is up.

  'Sara are you ready, I have to be at work soon,' my mother shouts up the stairs.

  'Coming mum,' I respond and take a last look in my long mirror, tipping it towards me slightly so I can see properly.

I'm prepared to face the world. I run down the stairs and out into the street and get into my mother's classic Beetle car. She smiles at me.

'Do your seat belt up,' I do as my mother advises, placing the bag with the red box on the floor by my feet. We're out onto the driveway and away.

'Say hello from me,' my mum says. 'You can stay for a few hours at the hospital, I double checked the visiting times.'

'Yes,' I say and smile a strained smile.

I still feel very disoriented as we drive up the winding roads and onto the busy dual Upper Bristol road, and on, until we get to a wooded area. My mother pulls up at the side of the road.

'Don't stray from the path and get the bus home, ring me when you're leaving, I'm only at work for a couple of hours this morning, I wish I was coming with you,' my mother says, she looks concerned.

I give my mum a kiss on the cheek and get out of the car, pick up my bag, and head towards the wooded area. There's a path through to get to the main entrance. The tall trees reach straight up to the sky. The branches stretch out and the leaves make a natural roof. The trees tower above me. I love trees. Everything feels better when you're surrounded by trees, or usually this is the case, I feel safe in the woods, but I haven't even felt safe here, my nightmares have represented this.

I listen and can hear the wind, and bird calls, these are multi-layered; a high-pitched whistle, a warble, notes in twos lowering in tone and chirping. Walking along, I notice a figure approaching me. It's a man; I recognise his stance from somewhere. He has his hood up and the sun is behind him, so it's hard to distinguish his features. He has on a T-shirt with a big picture of a grey and white wolf with orange eyes, this is more distinctive than his actual face. Wolves are beautiful creatures. They look like husky dogs. Wolves are extinct in England which makes me sad. But I suppose it is safer now.

'Hello,' the man says.

'Hello,' I reply.

'What are you doing walking through the woods by yourself?' he inquired in a nonchalant voice.

'I'm going to visit my partner in hospital, 'I say, openly and honestly, 'he's on Scarlet Ward.' I'm still confused by my dream of being in Bristol and don't even think to guard my words. There is also the possibility that this is a dream.

'Why don't you pick your partner some flowers,' he says and points to a patch of colour deep into the wooded area.

'Thanks,' I say, 'that'll be lovely,' and I head in the flower's direction, stepping off the path without hesitation; my mother's warnings are forgotten about. I walk happily through the trees and get to the patch of orange and purple flowers, picking a handful carefully. I didn't want to take too many because wildflowers are needed by bees.

The man quickly disappears into the distance. I walk happily through the trees, my bag in one hand containing the red box and a bunch of flowers in the other. The chimneys of the hospital come into view and soon I'm walking up the long drive and into the main entrance, passing people outside smoking in wheelchairs, and past the shops with cards and flowers, books, and sandwiches. I get to reception and am instructed to follow the red line on the floor until I get to Scarlet Ward. I pass men wheeling sick people on beds and patients walking in their nightgowns connected to drips. I see a couple crying.

Hospitals are strange places; they confront life and death every day and they're innumerable. What happens when you die? Has anyone witnessed anything of the Afterlife?
Did Death roam corridors waiting to guide the lost spirits to the light. Is Death an Angel? Could Death be sparkling white with a white hood, or red, roaming around in a red hooded cloak guiding people to follow along the path to a big house in the forest. I don't feel safe anywhere anymore.

I reach reception, a pretty nurse is sitting at a computer screen. She has on a blue and white tunic dress and her blonde hair is tied back in a bun. She smiles when she sees me, showing a mouth of perfect teeth.

'Hello,' I say timidly, I feel uncomfortable, 'I'm here to see my partner Mathew, I was told that I could visit him at this time.'

The solicitous nurse answers, 'yes that is fine.'

'A man came to see him earlier, he may be still with him, I was called away from my desk, so I'm not sure,' the nurse says and smiles, 'follow me. I'll take the flowers and put them in a vase. We aren't supposed to allow people to bring in flowers, but I will allow it this once,' the nurse says and smiles.

The woman gets up and takes me to a door and knocks.

'Come in,' a barely audible voice says.

'Go on in,' the nurse says and smiles, 'if you need anything, let me know, your sister will be so happy to see you, she's doing a lot better now,' the nurse rubs my arm, 'I'm Jane, just ring the buzzer if you need me.'

'Thanks, Jane,' I say and open the door hesitantly.

Inside, the curtains are closed. I see the outline of a person in the bed. They've the sheet pulled up, almost hiding their face. I feel elated. I'm going to see my partner. I haven't seen him for a year but maybe I dreamed of the year, maybe I'm mentally ill like my aunty. I go over to the windows and pull open the curtains and let the sunbeams into the plain room. I place my bag up on the table and remove the red box my mother had handed me. As I extract it, I realise that the box has multiplied into three, decreasing in size: the first medium size, the second smaller and thinner and the third smaller and thinner. Three Is The Magic Number. How unfathomable this is.

'Mathew,' I say.

'Come over here and sit on the bed,' a voice whispers, not sounding at all like Mathew.

I do, sitting on the edge and facing Mathew. The covers have been pulled down and I look at him. His face appears unrecognisable.

'Mathew, what a strange voice you have,' I say.

'All the better to greet you with,' the person answers.

'Mathew, what big eyes you have,' I say.

'All the better to see you with,' the person answers.

'What big hands you have,' I say.

'All the better to embrace you with,' the person answers.

'What a big mouth you have,' I say.

'All the better to eat you with,' the person says and jumps out of the bed and knocks me down, so I hit my head on the floor. I see the image of a wolf looming and I feel rugged hands holding me down and a mouth biting my neck. The shock wakes me up. I'm back with Innit in my room with fairy wallpaper, covered in sweat, back in reality. Or am I.

Chapter Twelve; The Truth

I still frequently feel numb to life and this has massively increased. I also feel strangely attached to Innit and must plan how to leave without hurting him. I am attached to heroin as well now. I am on the hamster wheel. I spent a few days recovering from my traumatic episode and waiting for the bruising to lessen. Innit has got me more Zanex, I take two every night and immediately fall asleep. If I dream, I don't remember; after two Zanex everything goes black until I awaken in the morning. I don't want any more nightmares; I've felt like my sanity is slipping away. My mind is fragile right now.

Between us we keep our habits going. I have started begging. I sit outside the Tescos slapping my face to stay alert. Innit no longer requires a bandage on his hand, the scab is frightful but is now healing in the open air. I have realised that I harbour strong feelings for Innit. I can't imagine not seeing his face every morning and don't know what I'm going to do. After dull days in the squat, we're at the weekend again. We'd stayed in and just scavenged for food. Innit has been very attentive. We discussed events with Kev but neither of us had any idea what had possessed him.

'It must be the Spice, in it,' Innit had said ruefully with sad eyes.

'Come on, I'll grab a bag and we can go get some free food, in it.' Innit has an empty rucksack and pulls me up from the sitting room floor. I grab my rucksack also. It's late Saturday afternoon and we're going up to the skip behind one of the local shops. We make our way down the hill. We'll have to carry the food back up again. And have a hit. I feel warm and cosy, full of energy. My pink-tinted sunglasses are firmly on.

We go left at the school, passing the road sign with a giant heart spray-painted on the wall above it. We pass the red brick wall which shimmers with anti-graffiti paint, like it's been dipped in wax. Passing the yellow sign and CCTV camera. We're enclosed by giant apartment buildings. Up the cobbled and tarmacked road, past the garages, one has a multi eyed green alien on, the other has a fox in boxing gloves and Jamaican coloured clothes, smoking a spliff. There are words painted here saying 'Cash Ruins Everything Around Us'; I don't think that is true. We pass a painting of a giant running hand and get to the metal spiked fencing of the supermarket car park. We've been watching out for Kev. Ironically, Innit possesses Kev's knife. Innit has not left my side all week and is now tightly clutching my hand as we walk up the alleyway.

We notice the familiar shape of Jay, waiting by one of the garages. His neat dreadlock hair in a ponytail as usual. A contrast from the unkempt dreadlocks of Squirrel. Jay's clean in comparison to the greasy unwashed Innit. Though since we've become involved, Innit washes more. We all stand by the graffitied garage and chat.

'Party on tonight,' Jay says.

'Where to Jay, in it.'

'At the warehouses on the other side of Bristol, by the river. You've been there before; you know where I mean Bruv.'

'Cool, Sara and I can walk, in it. We'll meet you there, in it.'

'Safe Bruv,' Jay smiles, 'I'll have some good stuff tonight, it'll have you flying.'

'Save us a wrap of Ketamine, in it.'

'I'll give you a freebie,' Jay replies. 'Safe Bruv, I like seeing you and Sara doing good Bruv,' Jay smiles, 'laters Fam.'

'Cool, in it, see you at the party later, Sara and I are going to raid the skip, in it.'

Jay is leaving and then turns back around and informs us, 'by the way, be careful, there was something on the Bristol news about some guy biting someone, or two people going insane and having to be shot as they were trying to cannibalise someone,' Jay looks disturbed. 'Freaked the fuck out of me when I saw it, Bruv, it's like the YouTube videos I saw of Spice addicts eating people in America, fucked right up.' Jay relaxes, 'Anyways, got to go somewhere, see you later,' Innit and Jay touch fists, 'safe,' Jay heads off.

I look aghast at Innit, he links arem with me. We go to the back of the local supermarket and open the bins and grab what we can, there's a caterpillar cake in there and a load of plastic boxed salads. Innit grabs them and stuffs them into his bag. I do the same until we can't fit anymore, we must be quick because we can get in trouble and there's a camera surveying the car park. I feel extremely fearful because of Kev the Chav. I'm scared all the time but having Innit with me makes all the difference. I cling to him.

When we arrive back home, we eat our food in Squirrel's room. Innit and I then go and lay down with a can of lager each, leaving Squirrel munching. We take Zanex and sleep. I'm getting too used to this life. Squirrel is going to stay in tonight and let us go out, he has a book on British plants to read.

When we awaken there are shadows in my room. Innit wants to go to the party to pick up the stuff off Jay, Jay also owes him some money according to Innit. I don't really feel like going but don't want to stay in without Innit. We bung on our clothes and shoes and headed out the door for the party venue. I bring my rucksack. We go out the house, seeing a little fox with a limp that walks along beside us and has me in awe. The fox darts behind a parked car on the road and we both wait for the fox to reappear, but it has gone, like a phantom. And down through Saint Paul's, passing the three maple trees with a huge neon banner saying 'SAVE OUR TREES', and down through the lit up underpass, someone has written 'Death is only the end if you only consider yourself' on the side of the tunnel. I suppose this quote is true, unless you believe in eternal life. Who would want that?

It's a waning moon. We get to the pelican crossing, bridging the busy main roads, and go past the big high-rises and down by the cycle path. We come out beside a posh, quiet, housing development. Passing a load of cranes at the back of the main train station and down a walkway with a green area which is covered in the dome tents in a circle. There is a rise in homelessness these days. Then past a Vauxhall forecourt with loads of flags advertising the make of car and past a Michelin garage with the Michelin man in the window. Innit points out an animal rescue centre, and we pass big factory forecourts; we can just see one is full up with massive bricks of recycled rubbish in the fading light.

We go through a factory forecourt with two parked vans which people obviously live in, and past a caravan, and come out on a main road by the River Avon. There are lit up billboards here advertising Netflix and MacDonald's. We go down the road and through another shadowy tunnel, I can just make out the words 'Eat the Tories' and a huge orange sausage dog painted down the side. We start to see people ambling along excitedly. We join them, having fun as we go with the other party goers; or as much fun as I'm able to have.

Passing another factory forecourt. Every big building or warehouse has fences of spikes, with razor wire or spikes, this is a spikey place. Then we turn into a big car park and see people hanging out of the warehouse windows. There's an orange-mandala-style-design on the window. Mandalas are meant to be depictions of God, so I read somewhere, this is curious because that would mean God is a representation of the natural patterns in life.

There's an atmosphere of excitement. We hear the music first and someone directs us to the entrance along the side of the warehouse, we follow a small path with beer cans on the ground until we come to a door and yank this open. A huge forecourt meets our eyes, we hear the beats echoing around the place and strobes are shooting out from on top of the wall of speakers. The happy crowd is dancing. As we weave in and out of the crowd looking for Jay, people dance on top of these speakers. We find him behind the Sound System by the DJ. Innit grabs the paper wrap of ketamine he wants. Using sign language to Jay because the music is so loud. We go and investigate. People are sitting all around the warehouse. Everyone looks ecstatic. There are vans and caravans parked up by the DJ. The shadowy walls are covered in graffiti. At one end is a big pile of rubbish, bits of wooden pallets and plywood are all piled up, there is even a roll of wrapping paper here.

We go up some stairs, past a window which has been covered by the canvas material of a tent, and into a room which has loads of people sitting down, hugging, laughing, chatting, and smiling. The floor's littered with silver canisters from the Nitrous Oxide gas and empty balloons and beer cans, empty water bottles, a lens off a pair of sunglasses, and there's even a book on the floor. There's an adjacent room, but the stud wall has been kicked through, leaving bare wooden beams and the furry wall inners coming out. People sit on the windowsills amongst empty bottles of spirits and other alcoholic beverages.

Innit and I sit down. Innit opens the wrap that Jay has provided him and places the white powder in the soft fleshy part between my finger and thumb. I sniff and sit back waiting to see what happens. Suddenly, I feel weird. I'm inside my own brain. Everyone feels like part of the same liquid and we're all flowing simultaneously. Straight after doing the ketamine, for one moment I think I'm about to stop and drift into nothing. I think I am dead. The fact that I'm still thinking makes me realise I'm still alive. I've no idea how long I've been in this room for. I'm still in shock from what happened and just want to be in the quiet with Innit.

I start to come around and can distinguish the lyrics of the song that's playing, 'I am a junglist soldier, fighting to keep the jungle alive'.

'Come on Sara, get up, in it.'

'I don't know if I can move,' I say and with that Innit heaves me up and puts his arm around my waist and we make our way downstairs to the dance floor. Trying not to step on anyone or bang into people on the way. Innit lets go of me and I manage to stay up. I dance. Every inch of me is in time with the music in a universal flow. People come up and talk for a bit or dance beside us, Init goes off and sees his friends but always returns to me quickly. People come up and talk or dance beside us, but I can't be bothered to speak to them. Innit goes off and sees his friends but always returns to me quickly. He takes me over to a man who's selling balloons, he's filling them up from a big bottle of gas which is taller than him. Innit buys us both a balloon and we suck in the contents, breathing in and out. One of Innit's friends comes over to us, a woman with pink hair.

'Sara, this DJ Angel of Chaos, in it,' Innit shouts an introduction.

The bright haired woman says, 'hi,' she smiles at me, 'I've been living in a vehicle on the road for twenty years, and mixing for that long... records... I'm old school. You can call me Angel.'

'Nice to meet you,' I shout back at her in a noncommittal way.

I can't be bothered to talk. I still feel lost. We go back and dance with this woman.

'I want to go for a wander, in it,' Innit says, 'you stay here with Angel.'

I dance, waiting for Innit to return. My rucksack is light because it hasn't got much stuff in, so dancing isn't that awkward. Angel wanders off. When Innit doesn't return, I start to roam around looking for Jay. I comb the warehouse, stopping to dance on occasions, but can't find Innit. The sun is rising so I can see because this is shining through the windows in the warehouse roof, the shadowy figures are becoming visible. Maybe Innit has gone? Maybe he couldn't find me? This is strange because I know Innit to be intrinsically loyal, he wouldn't just leave me. Not like my other partner. My mind starts to wander.

It's morning time; I'm thinking about my dead partner. I go to the entrance door, the door's small and you can't open it fully, and out along the path littered with beer cans. There are three-empty-green-wine-bottles here which reminds me of the song, 'if one green bottle should accidently fall...'. I notice that someone has written 'This is our church' on the outside wall and the words 'GOD IS A DJ'.

I need to search for Innit, so I go out onto the grounds. People are milling around in different states or sitting in their cars outside. I feel very low and at a loss. I feel guilty about my involvement with

Innit so quickly after my partner's death. He's dead and I'm just dancing the night away. Admittedly, I'd been through an extremely traumatic event. And where's Innit?

I want my partner, and best friend, here with me. I have done every day since his death. I sniffed that big line of Ketamine, Innit had given me a while ago, and this had sent me into a hole where my mind twisted and turned searching all my inner thoughts. I had no awareness of time or where I was until now. The effects are starting to wear off. My mind's thinking loads of different things. I'm left with the same idea; I don't want to be without my partner. I look around me at my surroundings; the metal fences around the factories and the jagged wire around the top, with black spiky balls that look almost mediaeval. Humanity can be cruel.

I suddenly see Jay and feel relieved, 'Jay, where's Innit, I can't find him.'

Jay joins me and gives me a hug he has a massive spliff, 'have some of this and chill, it's that Amsterdam shit, strong as fuck.' Jay hands me the spliff and I smoke it, it is very strong stuff, I can taste it. I feel slightly coerced into smoking it.

Jay takes the spliff back and says, 'Innit was going to find you about two hours ago, he was gonna do someting and I left him up against the warehouse wall over there, behind the green camper van, he's probably fallen asleep, Sara go and check it and I'll have a look inside, I won't leave until I know you are okay.' Jay smiles, 'meet you back in ten.'

'Thanks Jay,' I say.

'Safe Sara,' Jay responds and strides off in the direction of the warehouse.

I go behind the camper vans and see Innit's figure.

'Innit,' I say loudly but he doesn't answer.

As I get closer, I see that he is positioned weirdly. He appears as if he was sat up but has slumped down. He's white with a blue tinge. I stand above him. His head is on the floor, his arm is underneath his side and the arm of his sweatshirt top pulled up and there is a needle still protruding out of it. I've a weird feeling; I know he isn't asleep. I'm scared to touch him in case he feels cold. I stand for a minute, completely still, and concentrate on my breathing. I can do this. It takes all my courage to feel for a pulse. There isn't one. His eyes are closed. I kneel and gently open the lids of his eyes. They stay open and his eyes, like black holes, are transfixed. I lift his other arm and it drops down lifelessly.

Everything looks like him, his eyes, his nose, his mouth, his lips but it isn't him. Something has gone. He looks inanimate. Just skin. And blank. His soul has gone. The character of Innit is normally etched on his face but has now dissipated into nothing, like a shell that you put to your ear and can no longer hear the sea. The feeling of pure grief is overwhelming. Innit could just be asleep like I've seen him each morning for the last week, his breath consoling me. I stand up, turn around and walk away, saying goodbye in my head. If I walk away, then this might all evaporate? Innit might turn up? This could be a hallucination? I need to sit by myself.

I drift around to the side of the warehouse. Dazed. Not many cars have parked here. They didn't want to get boxed in. It is relatively empty. I see a couple a few metres away from me strolling to their car, hand in hand, and they get in and slam the doors. I look up and see the cloud drifting. The sky is grey. It looks so bright. Perfect. I now feel that today is a perfect day for an ending to my time. I've suffered everything I need to; I feel in a way like I have experienced God, but I don't answer to him; or any of the representations of the duality, or Yin Yan, which is life. I'd rather answer to John Lennon. At least I know he existed.

Hopefully Innit will be transfigured and so will I.

Music is playing in the background, and this is a constant tribal beat, like a heartbeat. It's probably what you hear in the womb as you take form, yours and mum's heartbeat replicating a dubstep tune. Maybe that's why I feel like returning home to the void, so I can be reborn. Or maybe I just have a death wish. I'm sitting in between two cars brushing my hands over the tarmac. The lasting effects of the drugs, lack of sleep and grief, have transformed this into a perfectly smooth surface. I can't feel the roughness grazing my fingers, but I can see the inflammation and tiny specks of blood on my pink hands. Flash backs to my harrowing rape enter my head. I need to clear my mind. I rise and wander around the abandoned warehouse grounds. I go behind the building.

I see a giant graffiti piece stretching across the wall and look in admiration, it's a depiction of the melting clocks by Salvador Dali; this is how my life feels to me now. Moss is growing at the bottom; nature always fights back. I can smell the damp. At this moment, this sprayed painting is extremely beautiful, more magnificent than the sunflowers and Irises of Vincent Van Gogh. Two dark purple trees frame the scene, shaded in with lighter and darker variations of the colour, the shading gives dimension to the picture, some of the leaves are very pale. I imagine melting into the picture and strolling in between the clocks.

I trace the signature in the corner with my fingers. I'm numb. I could lie on a bed of nails and not feel the nails pierce my back. Taking off my rucksack, I lean up against the wall. I'm alone and concealed. As I look down at the sparkling bits of glass from smashed bottles on the floor. I look up from the ground and see Innit's face hanging in the air before me like a hologram. I'd laid next to Innit for comfort and had listened to his breathing. I remember Innit. I'm tripping from lack of sleep and am dreaming whilst awake, or at least I think I am. I don't want to be alive anymore, not without my partner or Innit. I pick up a piece of glass and slice open my arm, the cut is deep, the hurt replaces the memory with pain. Innt is lifeless up against the warehouse wall. Being alive, I feel as if I'm the odd one out. All I need to do is inject shit loads of heroin. I hear Innit's voice in my head joking with me, 'I'm a heroin addict Sara, we don't last very long'.

I look up at the mauve sky hanging over me. I'm sitting on the floor, cross legged, and leaning against the wall. The sky is darkening. It will rain soon. I don't want to be here to feel the first fine spray of rain drops. Maybe I can smell and feel the rain for the last time and see the real dark grey. Tiny drops fall. I feel their soft weight and the cold in the air. I feel like the air is breathing. Everything is alive and buzzing like electricity. Too alive. Not real, just like a picture on a screen. My life feels like a dream. Everything I look at appears flat.

I return to Innit, I kneel on the floor sobbing and get my metaphorical pink-tinted sunglasses out from my sweatshirt pocket, undoing the arms, and place them on top of Innit's body like a head stone. Innit's is invaluable to me. I don't want to abandon him. I sit next to him, weeping inconsolably. I briskly walk away. The grey sky begins to pour down in torrents of rain. I trek for miles, the rain washes and rejuvenates me, and I keep going all day and all of the night. I see the spot lit face of the moon, the pin holes in space of the stars, and am still walking when dawn breaks the next day. I am sick as fuck and need to score.

I'm now firmly on the hamster wheel and if you want to find me, I'll be begging outside Tesco's. My veins in my arms collapse so I go in my groin and scar my arterial vein in my leg. I get an oozing infection and gain scars.

I want to be the Heroin of the story

Imagine thousands of tiny robotic spiders underneath your skin tickling every part of you. ATCHOO. If you could rip yourself open to reach the bone, nerve, vein and muscle below, you would. ATCHOO. I tried, they called it suicide. ATCHOO. You just want the incessant

131

itching, tinged with pain, to stop. There is a fine line. You can't stop the streaming tears dripping from your chin and the sneezing fits making your head spin. ATCHOO. The dame relentless feeling like an agonizing, unwanted orgasm is torture and will have you banging your head off walls. ATCHOO. Every molecule in your body is covered in fine hairs and is rubbing together, everyone seems to be laughing at the state you're in. You can't eat, drink or sleep, you can't even smoke a cigarette, and keep a bucket at hand, or a saucepan if there is nothing else. Uncomfortable thoughts keep popping into your mind like grazing your knee, or chalk scraping on a blackboard, and progressively get worse. Ceasing to exist would be a relief. ATCHOO. And all because you thought you could handle it, you can tell that to the families of the dead, sometimes the only way out of the cycle of addiction. ATCHOO. You are sat in a boiling hot bath, skin blistering and peeling to reveal goose bumps under each layer, cold as a stone surrounded by heavy snow. ATCHOO. ATCHOO. ATCHOO. ATCHOO

Can everyone wave their magic wands please and wish that I survive this. I now have three indelible and traumatic incidents scorched in my mind, like three red boxes increasing in size, these experiences necessitate therapy. At least life isn't boring, and thankfully after many years I would never partake in drugs again. What a life. Everything is so much better when you buzz naturally, you can have respect for yourself. The lyrics come into my mind; 'Here comes the sun, here comes the sun, And I say it's all right'.

What doesn't kill you, makes you stronger

Friedrich Nietzsche

It isn't about the drugs, it's about the music, in it.

Ananda Fox

Heaven

God sits on his swivel chair at his desk with his pot belly hanging out over his Y-fronts, gazing at his crystal ball and watching the Earth. His long mane of white hair flows down his back and his white moustache and beard obscure his face. He presses the button on his intercom to speak to his angel/secretary.

'Gabriel, come in here please, I'm annoyed and want to speak to you.'

Gabriel enters to a fanfare of golden trumpets, he's a stunningly gorgeous man, physique of a Greek statue, God's covering his ears and orders, 'tell the trumpeters to play quietly, I went out last night.'

Gabriel answers, 'I'm your humble servant. How may I assist you?'

'Come and sit down,' God commands, and Gabriel sits on the chair facing God, the scene out of the window is blissful. 'Right, Gabriel I got this answer phone message from a young woman on Earth called Sara, she's in difficulty by the sounds of it, why didn't you contact me, now she thinks that I don't answer. She's discrediting my name. I'm going to have to send Jesus down to save her, he won't be amused,' God shakes his head, 'he has only just got back from saving Barbara Smith, for god's sake Gabriel, see you have me blaspheming again, call yourself an angel, tut... tut... tut.' God glances at his crystal ball and then back at Gabriel, 'I told you to inform me of any urgent messages.'

Gabriel mumbles, looking at the floor, 'erm, sorry God. You could offer Jesus an inducement to give him some motivation; a day out with his mother Mary, they could feed the doves,' Gabriel looks up, 'this would be lovely for them.'

God smiles, 'you're right, get him on the phone.'

Gabriel passes God the solid gold telephone, a cordless one.

Jesus has just landed on the heaven's red carpet and is walking towards the control tower to clock in his work hours when an angel runs up to him with a phone.

'It's your father,' she says with high esteem and slight nervousness. The angel passes Jesus the phone and he raises this to his ear with slight reticence. He hears the familiar gruff voice of God.

-Jesus, we require you to go and save a young woman called Sara, can you go down to Earth. I'll give you some time off when you return to see your mother.

-Dad, my sandals have only just landed in Heaven.

-I know but it's imperative, Jesus.

-Dad have you seen it down there, masses of zombies, the Devil has created this flesh-eating thing. Hells too empty apparently, not enough staff to stoke the furnace, the temperature has decreased by two degrees.

- The Devil didn't clear that with me, you just can't work with him, he's incorrigible. Jesus, you know I wouldn't ask unless I really did need you.

-Okay Dad, as long as I don't get crucified again. You are The All Mighty after all.

I end with a poem,

LOVE

There's an invisible magnetism enabling the spark of creation which starts hearts to the world's clock, as the tides beat against earth and rock.

This emotion is like gravity which controls the universe, allowing me and you to mould together.

 parting would feel like the planets and stars having to realign, the sun ceasing to shine and night and day becoming linear time.

In the antithesis of life, our branches are entwined and the leaves photosynthesising, as my heart is
smiling.

The magnetic attraction, governed by the sun, holds everything in place, allowing everything to be.

And matter; you matter, I matter, we matter, US.

BLACK LIVES MATTER

God grant me the serenity, to accept the things I cannot change,
The courage to change the things I can, and the wisdom to know the difference,

Amen.

'Tis better to have loved and lost

Than never to have loved at all.'

Alfred Lord Tennyson